Lola Rising

Christina Whisler

Contents

Chapter 1

I just got back from work at the Twisted Bookstore, and now I am sitting at a corner table at my favorite coffee shop, Bean Their Done That. I have been coming to this shop and sitting at the same table for months. So, I am sitting at the same place I sat and eating and drinking the same thing every day I work. I see the same people every day also. So, when someone different comes in, you notice them.

I noticed right away when a new person came in, not only because he was a man but because he was so different that one would see anyway. And what I mean by different is that he exudes sensuality like no one else in the place did.

When he caught me staring at him, I looked away, hoping he had not noticed me looking at him. It was too late for that. He had seen, and when he was done ordering his food.

He walked towards my seat. “Can I sit here?” he asked. I felt that my heart beat faster than earlier.

“Y-yes,” I said.

He sat in front of me. “I'm Ben,” he said while smiling.

“I'm Lola,” I replied and smiled at him.

“Lola,” he said. His smile became even brighter. “I like that name. It is beautiful, and it suits you.”

I felt sweat in my palm. I looked at him directly, but on the inside, I was nervous. I felt overwhelmed that he appreciated me.

“How long have you been living in Los Angeles?” I asked him. I am not comfortable with the topic at hand. I became more nervous, so I changed the subject.

“Since childhood,” he said. “I came here to Earth from a different planet. I will tell you how I came to be on Earth sometime.

The corner of my lips moves upward as a little smile appears on my face. The way he talks about it is weird, but it is cute.

"You say that as you and I are a couple," I said as I laughed silently.

"That is because I intend on asking you out," he told me. "I want to get to know you better."

I was silent for a time; I even stopped laughing, and the way he said that made my heart beat faster again.

"How long have you been here in LA?" he asked. He wants a more extended conversation between us.

"Only a few months now.

I moved here with my aunt after my parents died in a car crash," I told him. "I live in the back of the house. I have a job at the bookstore across the street from here, so I come every day after work to unwind. As long as I have a job, I have a place to stay."

When I looked at him again, he looked at me with a possessiveness that I did not understand since we had just met. He was studying me when I started talking again.

"When did the accident happen?" he asked.

"In June," I said. Now, it was my turn to stare. I noticed everything about him. The way his muscles rippled when he moved. The color of his eye is what got me, though. His eyes were the color of liquid amethyst and reflected the heat and desire that he was feeling. His skin was dark from the sun, making his eyes stand out more.

I was lost in thought when he started talking again. "Earth to Lola." He said with a low chuckle that sounded like a low rumble.

"Oh, I was just thinking," I said.

He chuckled again with that low, sexy sound that sent goosebumps all over my body.

"Anything interesting?" he asked with a smile.

"I was thinking... Then I stopped." I started to blush, and he knew it was about him.

"What the hell is wrong with you," I asked myself as I gave myself a mental shake. He is just a man. I looked at my watch and said I must go home.

"Can we exchange numbers?" He asked.

"Yes," I said.

"He gave me his, and I gave him mine, and as soon as I was getting home, he was calling me. How did you know that I would be home?" "I didn't; I just waited for some time to pass by and decided to call you to make sure you got home okay."

"Besides, you ran out of here like you were on fire."

You forgot to say bye to me."

"Yes, I am okay," I said.

"When can I see you again?" I asked.

"When do you want to get together?" he asked.

"Is tomorrow okay with you?" I asked.

"Is eight in the evening good for you?" he asked.

"Sounds good to me," I said.

"Where would you like to meet up?" I asked.

"At the coffee shop where we first met is good for me."

"Okay," she said. Now I must go so I can get some sleep. I must work tomorrow morning. I will see you tomorrow evening."

I had just got home from work when Ben called. "I just got in the door," I said.

"I can't wait to see you tonight," I told her.

"Well, if we don't get off the phone, I won't have time to get ready."

"Okay, I will let you go." He said. I will see you at eight.

I hung up, showered, and prepared for my date with Ben.

I let my aunt know that I was going out and left to go to the coffee shop. When we met, we ordered food and returned to the car.

"Where are we going?" I asked.

"It's a surprise, he said."

The next thing I knew, we were at the beach. It was a beautiful night. We walked down to the beach area and took out a blanket to sit on the sand. He gave me my food and then took his food, and we started to eat.

The sun was setting, and it was such a beautiful site to see. It was so magical just being with Ben.

"I love the smell of the salty sea air," I told him.

"Me too, he said."

"It's late; give me your address, and I will drive you home." He said. I want you to take the bus on time at night.

"I am good with taking the bus," I said.

"I will not have you taking the bus anymore," I told her.

"Why?"

"It's not safe," I told her. That is my final word. I will take you to and back from work. I gave Ben my address so he could drop me off at home.

"You know, I can care for myself," I said.

"I know you can," I said. But I like this too much to let you take the bus.

"Why didn't you say that from the beginning?" I asked. I wanted to see how much I could push you before you gave in. By that time, we were at my place.

"Oh, you," I said and exited the car. Good night, Ben.

"Good night, Lola."

I went inside to say good night to my aunt and then went to my place in the back to go to bed. Sleep evaded me, though. I kept seeing Ben's face every time I closed my eyes. He is so damn gorgeous, and the way he smiles at me gives me goosebumps all over my body. I must go to work tomorrow morning. I wish I could go to sleep. I will go to work in the morning tired.

I was so tired that my boss told me to go home and get some sleep an hour into the workday. I don't have work tomorrow, so I intend to sleep in. Which is something I only get to do sometimes. Then Ben called.

"How did your day go?" he asked.

"Horrible, I said." I did not sleep well, and my boss sent me home an hour into the day. What was I supposed to tell him? I did not sleep because I was thinking about him all night. Yeah, right, like that is going to happen.

"Do you feel like going out to eat tonight?" He asked.

"I just want to sleep," I told him. I could tell he was a little disappointed, but he understood.

"I will call you tomorrow," he said.

"I plan on sleeping in tomorrow," I told him. Please call in the afternoon. Ben called me in the afternoon the next day.

Chapter 2

"How are you feeling?" he asked.

"Better," I said.

"Good," Do you want to go out to eat?

"Yes," I said.

"Great," I will pick you up in about an hour.

He picked me up, and we went for coffee and something to eat. Then we went to the beach again.

"Are you always so punctual?" I asked him.

"Yes," he said. "Does it bother you?"

"No, I was curious."

"Do you know how beautiful you are?"

"I do not consider myself beautiful." We were drinking some water, and he almost choked on it as I said it. "Are you serious? You are the most beautiful woman that I have seen in a long time?" "You have long wavy blond hair, Ice-blue eyes, milky white skin that shimmers like diamonds, and a body that most women would die for."

Now it was my time to choke on my water. "I never heard anyone describe me quite like that before."

"You haven't met the right person, then."

He kissed me hard, so hard that it left both of us breathless. We stayed quiet for a while. I was thinking about what just happened between us. Ben started talking first, and what he said blew me away. "I know it is only our second date, but I am starting to have serious feelings for you. I am becoming very protective of you." I did not give her a chance to answer.

"For now, let us get you home."

On our way home, we were quiet. I did not know what to say at this point. He made it clear that he was falling for me, and I just stared at him like a deer in headlights.

When we were near my place, my head was still reeling from what was said at the beach. I started to say something, but he stopped me.

"Don't think about it tonight." He said. Then dropped another bomb on me. "You are mine, mind, body, and soul."

"Do you understand?"

"Yes, I understand."

What else could I say?

Now, I am so confused. I could not say anything else.

"Just to let you know, I have not felt like this before I met you."

My jaw just dropped to the floor at this point. I started to protest, but Ben kissed me hard again. By the time we parted, my breath was coming out quickly. My head was reeling even more. I could not think; I just felt. I felt every nerve in my body come alive. My aunt was sleeping when I got home, so I didn't have to deal with her asking me questions about my appearance. I went straight through the house to mine in the back. When I got into my house and switched the light on, I could think better.

"Why did my body react this way when I am with Ben?" I asked myself. I don't know what to think right now. I looked in the mirror and saw my lips were red and swollen from Ben's kiss. My eyes are a shade darker. His claim over me had me hot for him, even though I did not want to admit it yet.

I showered and got ready for bed, but I still could not get Ben out of my head. I tried to get some sleep but could not. I took out my vibrator and tried to please myself, but that did not even work. When he said that I was his mind, body, and soul, he made it, so I craved him and only him. I could not stop thinking about him. We had another date; this time, we went to a movie. We sat at the back of the theater where no one could see us. It is like he was claiming me repeatedly with not only his words but also with his actions. I was aware of my whole body. I was on Fire.

It was a fire that I thought would consume me from the inside out. I felt incredibly hot and light at the same time. Ben kissed me, and when he ended the kiss, I just smiled at him.

"Are you having a fun time?" he asked.

"Yes," Thank you.

"Do you know what you do to me?" He leaned over and whispered in my ear. "You have me hard as a rock, and I want you with every fiber of my body."

I could tell she was blushing, even in the theater's darkness; I loved the way the color crept up her cheeks.

The movie was over. "Now, I must take you home before I do something I regret later."

When Ben and I were at my place, he told me that he had to go away on business.

"What do you do for work?"

"I own a ranch, which I must go to conventions once a year."

"Think about me when I am gone. I said.

"No," I teasingly said.

"I will call you when I get to my hotel," I said.

"Good night, Lola."

When I got home, I took a shower and packed my trip. I tried to settle in for the night, but I could not get to sleep. I could not get the image of Lola lying on her bed, masturbating at the thought of me.

I have fantasized about that ever since I saw her in the café.

Damn, she is going to be mine soon. I have to get some sleep. I have to be at the airport early in the morning.

When I got to the airport, I called Lola. "I will call you later."

"I have to work until eight tonight," I told him.

"I will call after nine." I wanted her to have time to eat and settle for the night. I had plans for my phone call tonight. That plan was to have phone sex with her. I knew once I had phone sex with her, she would be mine, and there would be no turning back for her. I would have her heart, mind, body, and soul. How do I know that? I just have a feeling. That's all. When I called her, she sounded tired.

"What are you doing?" I asked.

"I am in bed trying to get some sleep."

"I thought to myself, now is the time to strike."

"What are you wearing?"

"Nothing, I sleep naked." My jaw almost hit the floor with excitement.

"Good, now start touching yourself." I did what he asked of me and started to stroke myself all over my body without any hesitation. I heard her moan as she did so. Start playing with your clit. I want to listen to you moan.

"I am so hard I could explode," I told her. She moaned again, and I could tell that she was at her breaking point. I sat there, just listening to her moan.

Come for me, baby, he said in that low, sexy voice that drove me crazy, and that was all it took. I screamed out his name and came hard. I could hear her panting and trying to catch her breath. As I sat here listening to her panting, I lost all control and came with her, listening to me. We said our good nights and hung up the phone.

"Get some sleep," Lola said. I will call you tomorrow.

"I get off work at three tomorrow; you can call any time after that."

As I lay in bed trying to sleep, I thought about what had happened that night. I keep thinking to myself, what are you doing? I should not have let that happen; I don't do stuff like that. But damn, it feels so good to be a little wicked.

I was always a good girl.

Now, I feel like a bad girl, and it feels so good. I don't know how long I can hold him off. It is getting harder and harder to resist him. It's now the following day, and I am at work, and I can hardly concentrate on what I am doing. The day went by quickly, even though I had a tough time.

Ben called me after I got home from work, and I was at the cafe.

"How was your day?"

"It was okay, although I couldn't concentrate all day and was distracted by my thoughts."

"I will be home tomorrow morning. I would like to have dinner with you in the evening."

"Okay," I do not have to work, nor do I have any plans for anything else.

I had all day to make myself pretty for him, I thought to myself. He interrupted my thoughts.

"Wear something nice for me, preferably a dress.

"Okay," do you have a place in mind to go?

"Yes," be ready by eight.

"Okay," I said and hung up the phone.

It was now the following day, and I picked out the dress that I was going to wear. It was a black spaghetti strap dress that was close fitting. It was my favorite dress. I read some of the books that I had been reading before I got out of bed.

I was hungry, so I went to the main house to cook breakfast and say good morning to my aunt.

"I am going out again tonight," I said.

Then I went back to my place. I read some more of my book and then went to make some launch. This time, I ate with my aunt in the main house. Then, it was time to start getting ready to go out with Ben.

I took a shower and got ready for my date with Ben. I loved the way the dress hugged my curves. I did my hair and make-up, and then it was time to go. I was putting on my jacket when the phone rang. It was Ben, letting me know he was here.

"I will be out in a minute," I said. "I just have to let my aunt know that I am leaving. I went into the main house where my aunt was.

"I am leaving now," I said. Goodbye.

I could not see what Lola was wearing, but I couldn't wait to find out. Earlier in the day, I asked her what she was going to wear, and she told me that I was going to have to wait to find out.

When we got to the restaurant, I took off my jacket, and to my delight, he just stood there staring at me.

"Do you like what you see?"

"Yes," I said when I finally found my voice. You look stunning tonight."

"Thank you," I said with a smile.

He pulled out my chair so I could take my seat. Then he took his seat. We ordered two glasses of red wine and spaghetti. We ate, then headed to the beach to watch the sunset. As it was getting darker, we were still sitting on the beach. The tide was coming in, so we had to keep moving up the coast.

I leaned into her ear and whispered, "Take off your panties."

"I can't," I said as I blushed.

"Why," I asked.

"Because I am not wearing any."

"Fuck, Lola," you are killing me. I am so hard I cannot stand it.

"Now what?"

"Now, you will find out what I am all about." He said. I blushed again.

"I am going to kiss you now," I said.

He left me breathless and wanting more.

Chapter 3

"Open your legs," I want to hear you moan.

I do not know what it was about him, but I wanted to please him. I did what he asked, and he slipped his hand between my legs and started stroking my clit. I let out a moan and opened further for him.

As I continued to stroke her, her breath became faster, and she began to moan increasingly.

I whispered to her, "Don't cum." You can't make yourself orgasm until I tell you to. He drew his hand away. That means that you cannot make yourself come without me being there with you.

"Do you understand me?" I asked her.

I whimpered and said, "Yes."

"Yes, what," I asked.

"Yes, sir," I said. All the while, I thought, What the hell is wrong with you? I want to please a man I met a couple of weeks ago. Why can't I say no to Ben? It is like my body craves and cannot get enough of him.

It was late when I returned to the house, so my aunt was already sleeping. I crept through the house and went to my place. I was glad that she was not waiting for me. I was not in the mood to answer any questions that she might have. I showered and then went to bed. I tried to sleep, but I could not. I kept thinking about Ben and the way my body is now craving his touch.

Ben called the next day.

"Did you sleep well?"

"No," I did not sleep well. I could almost see Ben smile. He chuckled.

"Why is that?" he said in a low husky voice.

"Oh, you know why." My thoughts kept going to you and what you do to me.

"And what do I do to you?"

"I have no will to resist you anymore. My body craves you, and I find it harder and harder to resist."

"What is that supposed to mean?" I asked.

"You know what it means."

"I used to use my vibrator to get myself off, and now I cannot fucking get off anymore." I heard him gasp and thought to myself, I got him.

"I would like to watch you use your vibe on yourself." He said in that low, husky voice that drove me crazy and gave me goosebumps all over my body.

"I will see you later." He said and hung up the phone.

"What the hell is wrong with me."

Ben called again. "Can we eat at your place tonight?"

"Yes," I said.

"I will bring pizza and a movie.

"Okay," I said.

"I will be there at eight." I have the perfect movie to watch with you.

"What is the movie?"

"It's a surprise."

He arrived at eight with the pizza, movie, and a bottle of wine and the movie.

"Okay," what movie do you have for us to watch?"

He did not say a word; he just popped it into the player. When it started, I could not believe my eyes. It was a porn movie and not just a porn, but it was BDSM themed. I thought to myself, Holly Fuck!

"I never watched a porn movie before," I said.

"Get used to it; I watch them all the time."

"Let's eat," I said, gave her a slice of pizza and poured her a glass of wine. I did the same for myself.

After eating, she excused herself and went to the bathroom.

I made quick work to find her vibe and hide it only where I could see it. She came back into the room, and I had a devious smile.

"Take your clothes off," Ben said. One at a time and slowly. I want to watch you take them off and enjoy every inch of your body. Also, please don't take your eyes off mine while you are undressing. I want to see your eyes and how they come alive at the sight of me watching you. I did what he asked of me.

"So eager to please me, I like that." I rewarded her with a devious smile and her vibrator.

"How did you find my vibe?"

"There are not too many places you can hide things here."

"Well, what are you going to do with it?"

"What do you think I am going to do with it?" I am going to make you come hard with it.

She opened her mouth to protest, but I just shushed her.

"Come to me and kneel in front of me." At this point, she was nervous, but she did what I asked her to do.

"May I say something first?"

"Yes, you may."

"I haven't inserted the vibe, just putting on my clit was enough."

"So, you are my little virgin; thank you for letting me know."

I laughed nervously and said I may be innocent in my body, but my mind is quite the opposite. You know, I do read erotic romance novels.

"I will have to remember that you like to read. Thanks for letting me know that, too." I smiled inwardly and started to kiss her. I kissed her throat and worked my way down to her breast. I trailed little kisses down past her belly button down to her thighs.

"Part your legs so I can touch your clit with the vibe." She did what I asked, and then I slipped the vibe between her legs and started to stroke her with it. Lola let out a moan as she grabbed for me.

I heard Ben let out a moan as I clung to him.

It was the low, husky sound that made my heart faster.

She grabbed for me again, and this time, she let out a scream as she called out my name. She came hard; I let her come down off her orgasm high.

"Get on the bed," I told her.

"What are you going to do now?"

"Don't worry, that little head of yours, I am not going to fuck you yet. I am not done with you, though."

Chapter 4

"Now get on the bed." Lie on your back and put your knees up." I did what he told me to.

"Good girl," now spread those beautiful legs. I want to see all your beauty." She obeyed, and I rewarded her with another kiss and a smack on her ass. Kneeling between her thighs, I touched her clit with the vibe, and she came alive again. When she was close to the breaking point, I told her I would put my mouth on her.

"I want to taste you," I said.

At that point, I felt like I would go through the roof. When I came this time, it was like Ben was claiming me and branding me as his and only his.

When he was satisfied that I was spent, he crawled up beside me and hugged me.

"Good girl," you came twice for me tonight.

"Did you like what I did?"

"Are you kidding me? I loved it."

"Well, baby, that's just the beginning." "There is a lot more to it than that, and I am going to enjoy watching you blossom to my touch."

"I think I am going to like that too." She said as she smiled.

"You are mine and no one else." Do you understand me, Lola?

"Yes, sir."

I smiled, "you learn fast." I have to go to a meeting close by in the next town. I will pick you up after you get out of the meeting.

"What time do you get out?"

"Around three," I say.

"Okay," I will be there." He said as he went out the door, but not before planting a hard kiss on my swollen lips.

"Good night, good girl."

My meeting went longer than I thought it would, so I called Lola and told her that I was running late.

"Okay, meet me at the coffee shop then.

"Are you there now?"

"Yes, I will wait until you come and pick me up."

Ben showed up at the coffee shop thirty minutes later.

"Hi, he said with a smile."

"Tough day?" I asked her.

"Yes, it was a tough one for me today." Yet, I have an idea.

Why don't we go to the beach for a while, and we can talk about it? That sounds like a good idea. Just let me call my aunt to tell her I am going, and then we can leave. We arrived at the beach half an hour later. The sun was setting, and the sky was a beautiful pink and purple shade.

The tide was coming in, so we had to keep moving, but I did not mind because I was with Ben. I listened as Ben talked about his day, and at the end, when he was done talking, I asked him if he was feeling better.

"Just being next to you makes me feel better, Lola."

We went to eat something and then went to a movie. After the movie, Ben drove me home. We were at my place, still in the car.

"Good night, Lola," get some sleep. That's what I am going to do: get some sleep. I feel so tired tonight. Ben kissed me; good night.

With a smile, he said. "Now, please get out of my car before I take you here and now."

"I will call you tomorrow."

"Please call in the late morning. I don't have to work, and I am planning to sleep in." With that, I shut the car door. My aunt was in the kitchen when I came in.

"How did your date go, dear?"

"It went well; we went to the beach," and right now, all I want to do is take a shower and go to bed.

That is what I did. When my head hit the pillow, I was out like a light.

Ben called me in the afternoon the following day.

"Do you want to go to dinner?"

"Sure, I would love to."

"I will be there by eight, don't be late."

I was wearing a black A-lined dress this time. It hugged my breasts and pushed them up a little. We arrived at the restaurant and ordered two garden salads, vegan steaks, and wine.

"I had a good time with you last night."

"Well, it certainly seemed so.

"You know that sassy mouth of yours will get you into trouble one of these days.

"Is it now?" I said.

"You should keep it under control." He said with that low chuckle that sends goosebumps all over my body.

Smiling, I said, "What will you do about it?"

"If you don't, I will turn you over my knee and spank you until you do." She looked at me with a raised chin and a defiant look, and I chuckled again.

"Come on, let us eat before everything gets cold. We can discuss this matter at a later time. Lola chuckled low in her throat, and I almost lost control. I started to feel like I would lose control when I was with her. I was so drawn to her, and it was driving me insane.

Ben paid for dinner, and we left the restaurant to go to the beach to watch the sunset. We were sitting in the car, and suddenly, I had the urge to grab a fist full of her hair and kiss her hard.

When I pulled away, I saw the raw desire in her eyes, and I kissed her again. This time, when I broke the kiss, she looked at me and smiled. I wondered what was going through that mind of hers. I did not have long to find out; suddenly, she reached over and started to stroke my cock.

"Lola, right now, that is a very dangerous thing to do." She leaned over and whispered in my ear, "What's wrong? You can't take what you give out?"

"It is not that. It is because I find it harder and harder to go slow with you. And I want to go slow with you, but you keep doing stuff like you are doing now, and it's driving me crazy. Lola smiled again and unzipped my zipper and pulled out my cock, and started stroking it.

"What am I doing to drive you crazy?" I asked innocently.

I closed my eyes and let out a low, slow groan. Then her mouth goes around the head of my cock. I let her find her rhythm.

Holly shit, Lola That feels so good. With a pending orgasm on the horizon, I took a handful of her hair and shoved her head down my cock, and she greedily took all of me.

I groaned and said, "I am going to cum." She did not pull away like I thought she would. She kept going. I groaned one more time and came hard. When she was done, she sat up and smiled.

"I like how you taste." She said.

My cock stirred again.

"Shit, Lola, that felt good." We sat quietly for a few minutes.

“It’s late, Ben said.” I better get you home.

“I agree; I have to work early tomorrow morning.”

I have to leave for an emergency business meeting, and he said he would call me after work.

“Okay, be careful.”

“Don’t worry, I will.”

I went straight through the main house to my place in the back. I took a shower and went to bed. When I woke up, I realized that I had slept the whole night through. I did not wake up once. I took a shower and went to work. When I stepped into the house after work, Ben was calling me.

“Hey, what’s up?”

“Nothing much; I just wanted to let you know that I got to my meeting okay.”

Oh, okay, I just got home.“ I am planning on ordering food and then settling down to read. I have not been able to read in the last couple of days.

“Okay, I will call you tomorrow morning.”

“I have off tomorrow; you can call me any time during the day.

“Okay,” he said and hung up the phone.

I am getting brave, I thought to myself. Last night, I gave Ben a blow job in his car when there were a lot of people walking around. I ate and took a shower.

Chapter 5

Then I settled in with a book. I must have been reading for quite a while because when I looked out the window, it was dark.

I went to bed and slept all through the night again. When I woke up in the morning, I felt refreshed and ready to take on the day. I went into the main house to get some breakfast and then returned to my place and ate.

I had some cleaning to do. I returned my plate to the main house, washed it, and put it away. When I finished everything, I wore a pair of sweats and went to the gym. I signed up this past week. By the time I got back home, Ben was calling me.

"Hey, what's up."

"I am calling to see if you want to go to dinner after I get home tomorrow.

"Sounds good to me; I get out of work at three."

"Good, I will pick you up."

I was going to go to the gym after work but, since we are going to dinner tonight, we can spend the time before we go with each other.

"Are you sure you don't want to go to the gym?"

"Yes, I am sure."

"Okay, one more thing," Wear that black dress you wore the last time we went to dinner. I like that one the best and do not wear anything under it. I heard Lola gasp before she hung up the phone. The next day, I packed the black dress to take to work. When I finished the day, I changed at work and waited for Ben to pick me up.

We spent time together for a while before we went to dinner. The place we went to eat was on the sixth floor of the building, so we had to take the elevator. We ate our dinner, drank our wine, and then left. When we were in the elevator, Ben slid his hand up the back of my dress and started playing with my clit.

The elevator opened once to let some people in, and he stopped. When the door closed, and we were on the way back down, he started again. It is like he enjoyed the way this was making me feel.

He was also enjoying getting off on the fact we were doing this in a public place. Then, the elevator door opened, and everyone got out. We were in the car now.

"get in the car, Lola." I got in the car as he told me to. He also got in. "We aren't going anywhere right now."

I unzipped my pants and pulled my cock out as soon as I sat down, and started masturbating. "Lola, I want you to watch me." "I want you as hot for me as I am for you right now."

I just sat there in awe, watching him. I was so hot and hungry for him right then. "Holy fuck, Ben, I am so hot for you right now, I want to suck you off."

"Fuck, Lola, you are killing me." With that, he grabbed my head and forcefully put my face in his crotch.

"Then suck me however you want."

I greedily took him into my mouth and sucked him until he came into my mouth. When I was done, I sat up, wiped my mouth, and smiled.

"Now it's your turn, Lola. Spread your legs; I want to fuck you with my tongue." I did what he asked because I was so hot for him at the time that all I wanted was for him to give me a release. We had to get in the back seat of the car so we would have more room. He had the car door open, but I didn't care as long as he made me come. When he first touched me with his tongue, I thought that I was going to go through the roof. I was so sensitive to the touch. I moaned loudly. He kept going. I loved the way he felt against my pussy. I started to move with his rhythm, and it wasn't long before I was moaning loudly. There were lots of people around, but I didn't care. I liked that people were around us. It seemed to heighten the feeling that I was feeling.

After we were done, we got back in the front seat of the car and got out of there. "Fuck me, Ben, that was fucking good. I didn't expect that at all."

"Me either; let's get you home so you can get some sleep."

When Ben dropped me off at home, it was late, so my aunt was asleep. I had to be quiet as I went through the house. I took a shower and settled in for the night.

Ben warned me not to please myself, but I felt brave tonight. I set up my phone to record myself masturbating. I pushed the record button, removed my robe, and sat on the bed. I started to stroke my breasts very slowly, then went lower.

I stroked everywhere; then, I pinched my nipples. I parted my legs wide and started playing with my clit while I was still playing with my breasts with my other hand.

I felt myself growing closer to climax; I stroked faster and faster. My climax came crashing down on me as I screamed Ben's name.

When I was done, I checked if the recording was sound and sent it to Ben.

My phone dinged, and I saw that Lola sent me a message. I watched the video she had sent, and my cock instantly got hard. Damn, she is killing me. I warned her not to please herself without me being there. Now, it is time for her to discover what happens when she is disobedient. I called her in the morning.

"Hey, what's up?" She asked.

"Can you meet me at the coffee shop?"

"Yes, I will be there in half an hour," she said and hung up the phone.

We sat at a table in the coffee shop, eating what we had ordered; Ben sat quietly and watched me eat.

"I got your message last night." He said.

I looked up and said, "Did you like it?"

"Yes, but I warned you about pleasing yourself," did not I? Lola looked up at me and smiled wickedly, and I saw the desire in her eyes. I am going to have to punish you. You will not know when it is coming, but it will come. I saw the fire in her eyes and thought to myself, damn, she is doing this to get punished.

"Hey, I have an idea." I have to go to the ranch this weekend.

Chapter 6

Can you get off work and go with me? I remember you telling me that your parents had a farm before you had to come here. I want to take you horseback riding.

"I will let you know tomorrow after work. We ate the rest of our food and then went to a movie. Then Ben dropped me off at my place.

"Good night, Lola." He said and kissed me hard.

I left the car and went to my aunt's house. I said good night to my aunt.

"Why are you going to bed so early?" she asked.

"I have to open the bookshop tomorrow." I have to be at the shop early to get the shipment that is coming in. I also want to read a little before I go to bed. I went to my place, took a shower, and settled down to read the book I had been reading for the past couple of days. I only got a little reading done, though. I was still thinking about what Ben had said about my punishment.

I went to work early in the morning, and when my boss came in, I asked her if I could have the weekend off. I told her my boyfriend wanted me to go away with him for the weekend. I was friends with my boss, so I had no trouble telling her why I wanted time off.

"Cool, have a fun time."

"Are you sure?"

When I got home from work, I told my aunt I was going away with my boyfriend for the weekend. I could tell that she did not like it too much.

"Okay," she said and had fun.

I went into my house and called Ben. "Everything is good to go, and I could go with him this weekend." My boss said to have a fun time. "My aunt doesn't like it much, but she's overprotective.

"Okay, I will pick you up bright and early tomorrow morning."

"Okay, I usually get up at five in the morning anyway."

I packed my clothes and went to bed.

The following day, Ben was here to pick me up at six. We stopped for coffee and then left town.

"What did you pack?" he asked.

"A couple of dresses, jeans and sweatshirts, shoes, and boots."

"Good."

I smiled at him, "What did you pack?"

"I packed some dress clothes and some jeans and t-shirts, shoes, and boots."

We arrived at the ranch a couple of hours later. The place was beautiful. The mountains are covered with snow. The road leading up to the house was extended and stunning. The house was huge. It was white with black trimming. They have decorated the house with fall decor.

Everything smelled like cinnamon and apples.

I saw the horses and laughed with delight. "Oh, how I missed horseback riding and being on a farm." We got out of the car and entered the house, where everyone was happy to greet us.

Ben introduced me as his girlfriend, and I greeted everyone with a smile and a hello.

"I am Lola."

"Everyone seems nice," I said. Ben smiled and said. "That is because they are.

"I will show you to your room." He said.

"Okay. I want to freshen up a little anyway."

"Me too." He said. I will take you to see the horses later in the day.

"Okay, I am so excited to see them."

Chuckling, he said, "I know."

We went to see the horses, and she loved being with them. I could get used to this, I thought to myself. Seeing her with them, she looked at home. I love watching her. Just the sight of her made me hard. She chose her horse, and so did I. We went riding through the trails by the house. We hit a clearing in the woods, and I heard her gasp. It is so beautiful here. I love the snow-covered mountains.

"They are breathtaking." She said as she came up alongside me.

"This is my favorite spot," I said.

"It's so peaceful here." She said.

We returned to the stalls and put the horses away for the night. Did you like riding again after all the time away from it?

"It felt good to ride again." She said. I have not been riding since I have been in California. I miss it and everything about being on a farm. I loved going to the clearing. It is romantic to me.

I smiled at her and said, "You think so."

We went into the house after we were done putting the horses away. I made some hot chocolate for us, and then we sat by the fireplace. We drank our chocolate silently, and when we got done, I tried to talk about her parents some more.

There is not much to say about them. I do not know that much about what happened to them. I only know what I know because my aunt told me some of what she knows. I believe she knows more than what she has let on, though. One day, I will ask again, and I will ask her to tell me the truth. All my aunt had said was that they were born and raised in the same town and were school sweethearts. They married and had me. Then, later in my life, they died in a car crash. For some reason, that didn't sit well with me, and I thought that she was making the story up. I know she is not telling me the truth, and it doesn't feel good.

"Maybe she thinks that she is protecting you."

"Maybe, but it still doesn't feel good to me, and it doesn't feel like she has told me everything she knows."

Something is wrong about what she has told me, and she is not telling me everything. Lola was half asleep when I heard her mumble, I love you. I loved the sound of her saying it. It made my heart sing. There is no turning back for her. I had the feeling that she did not want to turn back anyway. When she woke up, I was still by her side, watching her sleep.

She sat up and said, "Thank you for bringing me here." I needed this. I love it here.

"When you come up again, I would like to come too," I said.

"You are welcome to come up any time you want," I told her. This place has been in my family for generations, and my sister and I oversee it.

"I thought you said you arrived here as a child?"

"I did," I said. Some of my family chose to come here years ago.

"Lola, there is still the question of your punishment." He said.

"You didn't think that I forgot it, did you?"

"I did think that." She smiled the biggest and brightest smile she could. We are first going to dinner; I am hungry.

"Where are we going," I asked.

"It's a surprise. Now go get dressed into something sexy, would you," Ben said, walking me to my room. "One more thing, don't wear anything underneath the dress."

"Are you kidding me? It's freezing out."

"Just do it, Lola."

We went to this quaint little diner in the middle of nowhere. What seemed like it took hours to get there. I had a salad and a glass of wine, and Ben had a veggie stake, some veggies, and a glass of wine.

"Why is the dinner empty?"

"I rented it for the night."

I did not want anyone else here when I delivered your punishment. I looked up at Ben and said, "You wouldn't, Would you?" He gave me the wickedest smile he could.

"Yes, I would now come over here.

"What about the other people that are here?"

I paid them well; they will not be bothering us.

"Now, come here."

When she does not move, I will only say it one more time before I drag you over here.

"Now, come over here." Come here in front of me. I did what he asked of me.

"Kneel," he said, and I did. He was watching me. He scooted away from the table. Now, get up and bend over my knee. I did what he asked.

"I am going to spank you now."

I braced for the first strike, and when it did, I did not expect to feel what I did. I felt the sting of the hit, but it also felt good.

"Did it feel good?" I asked her.

"I could not answer; I could only feel." He gave me a couple more smacks, and then he was done. He patted my ass and made sure I was okay. Then he told me to go back to my seat. I did as he told me to do.

"Do you know why I punished you?"

"You did it because I pleased myself without you."

"Yes, and what did I tell you about doing that?"

"You told me I couldn't please myself without you being with me." As we drove back to the ranch, he asked how I felt about being spanked.

"I am confused about how I feel about it. I know I liked it, but I feel like I am not supposed to like it." "I guess I am feeling depraved."

"There is nothing to feel depraved about. It is okay that you like it. You should not feel ashamed in any way because you liked it. I like that you liked that I spanked you. You should know that I would never do anything that you do not want to do."

I saw the desire still in her eyes, and I could not help myself. I reached over and put my hand between her legs, and started to play with her clit.

My head fell back as I opened wider to let him in.

"Lola, come for me, baby." I let out a loud moan and came. We turned down the road to the house.

"Thank you," I said.

"Thank you for what?" he asked.

"Thank you for letting me come." She said.

"You're welcome," I said.

It was late when we arrived back at the house, so I walked Lola to her room. "Remember, you are not to please yourself without me being with you." I looked at him with a smile.

"Would you like to come in?"

"Not tonight, Lola; you know that I want to go slow with you."

"You can't blame me for trying, can you?"

I chuckled and said, "Lola, go to bed; we must leave early to return to LA."

"Wait here, Lola, I have something for you." He came back within a few minutes. I bought you this.

"What is it?'

"It's a book." You might like it. Read it when we get back to LA. Right now, please get some sleep."

When it was time to go, we said goodbye to everyone and left to go back home to LA.

We arrived in LA around dinner time, so we went to eat something, and then he dropped me at home. When I went to get out of the car, he stopped me and kissed me hard, so hard it seared my soul.

"Now, I can say without a doubt that I have been soul fucked."

"Get some sleep tonight, Lola."

"Do you have to work tomorrow?" I asked her.

"Yes, but in the morning," I said.

"Okay, I will be there to pick you up." You know I want you to avoid taking the bus.

"Okay, I said and left to go into the house.

"Okay, I said and left to go into the house. I took a shower and went to bed. The following day, I was getting ready to take a break from work, and Ben called."

I was around, and I wanted to know what time I could pick you up?"

"I am on break now if you want to come by the coffee shop. Otherwise, about one in the afternoon would be great."

"Okay, great, I will be there in a minute." How is your day going so far?

It is slow at the bookstore today.

"That is why I am on a break. I must go back in five minutes, though."

"While I am here. I want to meet your boss. I want to introduce you to her. How would you like to come to the bookshop when I get off today? I will do it then.

"I would love to."

Well, I must go back now, but come by the store when I get off, and I will introduce you to her.

"I will see you then. I will order some food, and we can go to your place to eat."

"Okay, I will also introduce you to my aunt. She has been asking about you."

Ben arrived at the bookstore just as I was getting out. We said hi to my boss, and I introduced Ben to her. This is my boyfriend, Ben. Ben, this is my boss, Sue.

"Lola, are you done with work?" I have the food in the car.

"Yes, I am done for the day." Bye Sue, I will see you soon. Then we left to go to my place. We got into the car. OH god, That food smells so good. I cannot wait to eat. I am famished.

"What did you get?"

"It's a surprise," I have a movie too.

"I hope it's not another porn movie."

"No, this time it's a romantic movie."

When we got to my place, we went into the main house so I could introduce Ben to my aunt. We went into the kitchen, where my aunt was cooking something for herself to eat. Auntie, I want to introduce you to my boyfriend. Ben, this is my aunt. Auntie, this is Ben.

Sorry to be short with the introductions; I am hungry. We went to my place in the back and ate our dinner. While we were eating, Ben asked me if I wanted to go back to the ranch someday.

"Yes, I do," I said.

I want to go back. I love animals and understand them somehow. I love being there. For now, I must stick around here and work. Speaking of work, I must go in late in the afternoon tomorrow.

"What time do you get out?" Ben asked.

"Nine, I said."

"Okay, I will pick you up. I must go now, see you tomorrow. I walked Ben to his car.

"Good night, I said."

"Good night, Lola." I went back to my place and went to bed.

It is now the following day, and I am at work and on my break. This girl came up to me and started talking to me. She was friendly, so I liked her instantly. She introduced herself as Shiloh. She's dressed like a punk rocker. Even though she is nice, she has that punk rocker attitude to match how she dresses.

She told me her parents were wealthy, so she did not have to work. In my mind, she is a spoiled little brat but likable though.

Her hair is black and styled in a mohawk. She wears black clothing like ripped jeans and a band t-shirt, a black leather jacket, and leather bracelets and a belt. She also wore black eyeliner. Right away, she started telling me things about Ben.

"How do you know Ben?"

"We dated for a while."

"How do you know that I am with Ben?"

"I have been watching you guys for a while."

"Why?" I asked.

"It gave me something to do."

"Don't you think that's a little creepy?"

"No."

You know Ben Is not what he seems. Shiloh told me that Ben's sexual desires are hard to deal with. He has BDSM tendencies. She went on to say that Ben likes women as submissive only. She also told me that when he tires of a woman, he leaves them. He will leave you, too. He left me. I guess when I said to him that I had fallen in love with him and I wanted more out of our relationship, he decided to beat me and leave me. He does not want a committed relationship. I do not want the same thing to happen to you. Lola just sat and listened to Shiloh talk.

I did not necessarily believe everything she told me. Still, some of it made sense without letting Shiloh know what was happening in my head. I excused myself by letting her know that I had to get back to work and that I would talk to her later.

I called Ben and asked if we could talk.

"Sure, I will pick you up after work.

"Okay," I say.

"What's going on, Lola?"

"Something we should talk about privately."

When Ben arrived, I was a nervous wreck. What is going on? I can tell something is truly bothering you. Well, I met this girl today, and she told me things about you. She said she knew you.

"What's her name?"

"Shiloh," I said.

Oh Shit, Lola, she is nothing but trouble. She has broken up every relationship I have had in the last year. She wants to get back to me.

"What did she say to you?"

She came to me acting friendly. She introduced herself and everything. Then she started to tell me that you are not what you seem. That you only want submissive women. When you tire of them, you leave them. She told me that when she said to you that she loved you and wanted more out of the relationship, you beat her and left.

I am so sorry, Lola. She has been telling everyone that that is what happened. It is not valid. Well, at least the beating and leaving part is not. I do like my women submissive, but I do not beat and leave them.

"Why in the world did you pick me to date?" I am not submissive.

I can tell if a woman is submissive or not. When I started dating you, I assessed you. Do you remember?

"Yes," I said.

"That is how I know. You are submissive, but you do not know it yet. You know I will never do anything to hurt you.

"I know; I just wish you would tell me this. It would sound better coming from you than someone I do not know."

"I will from now on. Is there anything else you want to know?"

"Yes, I would like to know where you came from?"

"Ah, that question again? Are you sure you want to know?

"Yes," I said.

Well, I came from a different planet. My parents sent me here. I did not want to come, but my parents made me go and stay with my family here on Earth. You see, my planet was at war. The overlords took total control of the planet. So, I am here along with my brother, whom I have not seen in years. So, that is the story. We can blend in with humans because we have the same skin type. The only thing that does not change is our eye color.

"That explains a lot." Thank you, I am glad that is out of the way. I believe you, but in the future, please come to me and let me know these things. My head is spinning, but I am glad you told me. It sounds better coming from you. The next time she comes up to me, what do you want me to do? Just be nice to her. Keep her from knowing that we talked. I want to see if she is in contact with my brother. She might be because he likes the weird ones. Plus, he is as evil as the day is long.

"Is there anything else she said to you?"

"Yes," she told me that she had been watching us for a while now.

"Jeeze, that's creepy." Now, I know that she is connected to my brother somehow. For now, do not let this bother you. Let us talk about something else.

"Okay."

I love being at the ranch this weekend. I loved it so much I cannot wait to go back. I am glad you feel that way because I want you there whenever I go. I hope your boss is okay with it. I will talk to her and let you know.

"I have an idea," Why don't you ask her to come to dinner with us tonight?

"Okay," give me a minute. I will be right back. Sue said she could not do it tonight, but the weekend would be better for her.

Chapter 7

"Okay," set it up then. I will talk to my boss tomorrow. After the day that I had today, I want to relax.

"Can we go to the beach?"

"Sure, we can," let us order something to eat first, and then we can go. I am starving.

"What do you want to eat?"

"I am not hungry, so I just want a coffee."

"Are you sure," I'm going to have a sandwich and coffee.

"Yeah, I am sure." I have lost my appetite today. I will call my aunt to let her know that I am going to be with you, and I will be late coming home.

We ordered what we wanted and went to the beach. It was late, so the sun had already set, and it was dark. I needed this. There is nothing like the salty sea air of the sea; it calms me down.

"So, when can I go back to the ranch?"

"Whenever you want. How about this weekend after we get done with dinner?"

"Sounds good to me."

Let us get you home before your aunt has a cow. I get the feeling that she does not like me much. I do not think that is it; she is very protective of me.

Ben took me home and dropped me off. "Lola, try and get some sleep."

"Goodnight, Lola."

I have to work tomorrow; I will set everything up with my boss to go to dinner. I went into the main house, and my aunt was still up.

"Did you have a good time tonight?" my aunt asked.

"Yes, I went to the beach to relax." I had a rough day today. I want to go to bed. Sorry, Auntie, I do not want to talk right now."

"That's Okay, just go and get some sleep."

I went to my place and took a shower. When I hit the pillow, I was out like a light. I went to work the following morning, hoping that this day would be better. It was a little better, but Shiloh was still hanging around.

I wish she would not hang around this much. She makes me nervous. She has not said anything to me all day. It is like she is a fly on the wall.

I called Ben and told him that dinner was a go on Saturday.

"Okay, good."

The week flew by so quickly that I did not notice if anything bothered me. It was Saturday before I knew it. I packed my clothes so I could go to the ranch with Ben. We met Sue at the diner and ordered our food and drinks. We ate and laughed at the silliest stuff. When it was time to go, I approached my boss about going away with Ben again. She was okay with it because she was also going away for the long weekend. It was a holiday weekend. It was time for us to go; we said our goodbyes, gave hugs and went on our way to the ranch.

When we finally made it to the ranch, it was late, so we went quietly into the house. Ben walked me to my room and kissed me hard.

"Good night, Lola."

I smiled at him. Are you sure you don't want to come in?

Lola, you are killing me. It is late, get some sleep. We will go riding tomorrow morning.

The morning came, and there was fresh snow on the ground. We went to the stables and hooked the horses to a slay and went for a sleigh riding through the woods and were at the clearing in no time. I took a big breath in. I love it here. It feels so freeing here. Like I do not have to worry about anything. I love that feeling. I wish I could stay here forever.

You can if you want. I will talk to my sister to see if it is okay.

I thought you said you owned the ranch.

I did; I like running things by my sister first. I will talk to her later.

I would love to live here; thank you.

It was cold, but I loved it. We stayed at the clearing for a while, just talking about anything and everything. It was beautiful, and I loved talking to Ben.

It was afternoon before we arrived back at the house. I was so cold that I was shaking. Ben made some hot chocolate, and we sat by the fire and drank it. The house smelled like cinnamon and apples. Now hot chocolate.

Lola, why don't you go and take a nice hot bath? I will talk to my sister about you moving up here.

Okay, I will be back down in a little while.

Take your time and leave the door unlocked. I will be up to dry you off.

Okay, I said.

I went to my room, drew my bath, and got into the water. It felt so good to take a bath instead of a shower. I wanted to stay in, but I heard Ben call out to me. Lola, are you done, or do you want me to wait a little longer?

"No, you can come in." Ben started drying me off from head to toe. He took his time and stroked every inch of my body. When Ben was done, he carried me to the bed and sat me down.

"I will be waiting for you downstairs. Get dressed. I am hungry and want to go out to dinner. It is cold out, so dress warm. I got dressed and went downstairs.

"I am ready. Do you have a place in mind to eat at?"

He leaned into me and said, do you remember the place I took you to where I punished you?

"Yes, I said. "

"That's the place we are going to tonight. It is one of my favorite places to eat." I blushed, and he knew that I was thinking about that night. "

I love how you blush when I talk dirty to you, even though I was not talking dirty just then. You remember, and that is a good thing."

"We were having dinner tonight because we are having Christmas dinner here tomorrow night, and the next day, we must be on our way down to LA. "

It would be best if you told your boss and your aunt that you are moving up here. I started to giggle and jump around like a little girl.

Thank you, I said.

In times like this, I would love to throw her over my shoulder and bury myself in her.

"Okay, okay, let us go."

"Are you always so punctual?"

"Why does it bother you?"

"No, I am curious."

"I have never been late for anything in my life that I know of."

When we arrived back at the house, it was late. So, everyone was sleeping. Ben walked me to my room, but this time, he came in with me. He shut the door and pinned me against it.

"I am starting to lose it with you. My self-control is slipping." I trapped her body between the door and me. I had her hands high above her head. I did not stop there; I shoved my up her shirt and started playing with her breast. I pulled on her nipples, and she leaned into me. With one knee, I spread her legs apart, and with my now free hand, I played with her clit.

I whispered in her ear. "Nothing underneath, just how I like you." She almost lost all control. I pulled away breathlessly and said not yet, love, not yet."

I was as breathless as he was.

I whispered, "Why not now?"

"Because I want you to do it just as bad as I do. I want you to beg for it first." I knew she was at the breaking point, but I wanted to find out how much she could take. I also knew that something was holding her back from letting go. I know she is submissive at heart, but she is not ready to give in yet, which is one of the things I love the most about her.

I want her to want me so wrong that she cannot say no. Plus, we have only been dating for a couple of months, and I am old-fashioned when it comes right down to it. I could have easily had her at once, but it would not have been right for her.

"Go to bed and get some sleep; we must leave in the afternoon tomorrow." I left her room and closed the door, but I did not move for a few minutes. I was trying to collect myself before I went to my room. Damn, she is killing me, I thought to myself. God, I want her so bad. I went to my room, lay on my bed, and tried to get some sleep, but I could not sleep.

I kept seeing Lola in the state of desire that I had put her in and instantly got rock-hard at the thought. I imagined how it would be to be inside her. When I finally got to sleep, it was time to get up and take Lola for her last sleigh ride before we left this afternoon.

It's funny; we have only been dating for a few months, but I have fallen for her. I wanted to make her happy. I woke her up, took her to the stables, tethered the horses to the sleigh, and went on our way to the clearing that she loved so much. I packed some hot chocolate so we could have something warm to drink.

I feel at peace here. I cannot explain it, but it feels like I am at home here.

"I cannot wait for the day you are up here for good. I do not like the city."

"Out of curiosity, "why don't you like the city?"

"It reminds me of where I am from he said and dropped the conversation. From the look on his face, I knew not to push it. I felt for him, though. I missed the place I came from, too.

"If you want, I will take you back to Montanan for vacation when ready. I made her cry. I am sorry for making you cry."

"That is okay; I am still grieving over my parents."

"Still, I do not like to see you like this, and I do not like to see you hurting like this. Let us see if we can take your mind off it." I tugged on the reins and the horses, and they began to move again. We went deeper into the woods. I asked her if she had ever been fishing.

"No, she said."

"Would you like to learn how to Ice-fish?"

"Yes, but this will make us late leaving here.

"Can you call your boss to see if you can stay an extra day or two?"

"Yes, I will do it when we return to the house." We stopped in front of a small shed and took her in. There were some fishing poles in the corner and a hole cut out in the middle of the shed.

"Could you grab two of the poles and come to me?" I took one of the poles, and she took the other. I put bait on both hooks and gave one of them to Lola. I had the other. Both of us put our poles in the water. Lola asked me again where I came from. "

Sorry, Lola, I cannot talk about it yet. I will tell you when I am ready. Someday, I will tell you. Right now, I need you to understand that I cannot discuss it."

I quickly changed the subject. Did I ever tell you that I have a dog?

"No, but I love dogs."

"My dog's name is Peppie."

"That is a cute name for a dog. I am glad you like it." My aunt keeps him in her house because my place is too small for a dog. Do you think your sister will let me bring him?"

"She loves dogs, so I think it will be okay."

Lola felt a tug on her line and got so excited that she screamed, I got one. I just chuckled at her and said, "You certainly did." I helped her get it off the hook, and she looked at it and threw it back in the water. To see what she would say, I asked her why she threw the fish back into the water.

"That is where it belongs. Animals are our friends and not meant to be eaten."

"It is getting late. Let us get back to the house." We got back into the sleigh and started returning to the house.

When we returned, we went straight into the house and let one of the groundskeepers take care of the horses and sleigh.

The scent of pine hit me like a rock. I have always loved the scent of pine; it smells so earthy. I looked up, and we were standing under a mistletoe. As I was standing there, I told him to look up.

He looked up, smiled at me, and said, "This means I must kiss you now." He did precisely that; he kissed me hard. When we broke the kiss, I felt like my head was spinning. With that in mind, I said, "You know, you make my head spin.

He chuckled and said, "That is the point. You know, you do the same to me." You know, Lola, one day we will be alone, and I will make you beg for me and scream my name. She bit her lip, got on her tippy toes, and whispered in his ear, "That sounds good," and I got hard instantly.

"You, my dear girl, are killing me."

She chuckled and said, "What is good for the goose is good for the gander."

Ben walked me to my room and kissed me. Before I entered my room, he smacked me on my ass and told me I was being a naughty little girl. I do not know why that excited me; it did for him to tell me it was like setting me on flames. I felt lightheaded, and I felt a rush of liquid heat between my legs. He makes me feel like no other man could. It is not like I have not met men before.

I just have not met anyone that when he walks into the room, and I get instantly turned on. He makes me feel sexy, wanted, and like a queen when I am with him. I could get used to this.

The man was everything to me, but how could I tell him that? We have only been dating for a few months, and it is too soon to say how I feel. I am afraid I might scare him away. Oh, what am I to do? If I tell him how I feel. I run the risk of losing him. I cannot tell him yet; he will think I am crazy and leave me. This week went too fast; today is Christmas day, and we were opening gifts. Ben got me a necklace and earring set and a book.

Do you like your gifts?

Yes, I said.

For me, the time was going too fast. I want to stay longer. I talked to my boss, and she is okay with me staying an extra day, but it is still not enough. I had a long day and wanted to sleep. Ben walked me to my room and asked me if something was wrong.

This week went so fast. I want more time. My boss gave me an extra day, but I still need more. Plus, he cut me off by saying, "Wait a minute, you have been wearing that hat all day, and I know that you don't like wearing it."

"What is with it?

"Promise you will not laugh."

"I won't laugh."

"Here goes; when I woke up this morning, I had these."

"You had what?"

"Look at my ears; they're pointed." I pulled off my hat and showed him my ears.

"Does it bother you?"

'Yes."

"Why?"

"Because I do not know why it happened. When I return home, I must talk to my aunt about this. She is holding something from me, I am sure of it. Then changed the subject."

"I don't have much to pack when I get home. The furniture is all my aunt's. I have to give my boss my two weeks' notice." I went into my room. I was so beat, I did not even change my clothes. I laid down on the bed and went right to sleep. I did not wake up until morning. "If this is what I get when I am here, then I know I will love living here. I know you will be here every weekend then."

"With a chuckle, he said yes, I would.

"I explained to my sister about your situation, and she said she would be glad to have you and your dog here. So do not worry about anything." I hugged him and said, "Thank you. I will give my notice at work."

"I am happy that you are happy. I want to see you happy. I cannot bear to see sad anymore."

The day went by quickly; before I knew it, we left to return to LA. When I returned, I gave my two weeks' notice at my job. I told my boss I had the opportunity to work at the ranch. I thought she would be sad to see me go, but she was happy I found something I loved doing. She just said to visit occasionally. I told her that I would. Now, I must go home and talk to my aunt. I know in my heart that she is holding something from me. When I got home and went in. I called to my aunt. She yelled from the kitchen,

"In here, dear."

"I need to talk to you."

"That does not sound good."

"Look, auntie, I am going to ask you once. What is going on with me?" My aunt looked stunned.

"What do you mean dear?"

I took off my hat and showered my ears.

"There are just ears dear."

"No, I said they are pointed and not normal ears. It just happened this week."

"I knew this day would come; I did not think it would come this soon.

You should sit down for this, my dear. Your mother was not what you call normal either. She was from the fay world. Your grandmother is the queen of the fay witches. Her name is Morgan LaFay. Your father was from the mundane or physical world.

Your mother met your father here and decided to marry him. The Fae world is not all as nice as cotton candy. After your mother was married to your father, she was excommunicated, and they were hunted down".

"You see, your mother was thought to be a trader to her people and their world because she married a man from the mundane world. She was willing to disobey their laws.

Your mother begged me not to tell you until it was necessary.

Dear girl, I hoped it would not come to this."

"So, what are you telling me?"

"I am telling you that you are a halfling. Half human and half fay."

"Holy Shit!"

"Your mother had powers too."

"What do you mean by powers? Please tell me."

"Your mother had the power of healing. That is how the fay knew where to look for them. They knew where she was whenever she used her powers to heal. You have those powers. She gave you those same powers at birth."

"Are you telling me that my mother was a fairy?"

"Yes, that is exactly what I am telling you." You have to know that being who she was wasn't easy for her and your father, and after having you, it was even more challenging because they knew that they had to protect you at all costs.

Please, dear girl, be careful when using your powers. They will come after you, just as they did your parents. They think of you as tainted blood. That was not an ordinary incident that your parents were in. Morgan's cronies killed them.

"Auntie, there is something else I must talk to you about. I have a job opportunity up at the ranch. I am moving up there tomorrow morning. I already gave my notice at work two weeks ago. My aunt, of course, tried to give me a rough time about it."

"Look, Auntie, I am old enough to make my own choices, and I appreciate everything you have done for me." I don't like moving far away from you, but I hate the city and miss being on a farm."

"I know you are a girl. I want you to be careful. I worry about you. I am just looking out for you."

"I know, Auntie, and I am glad that you were here for me when I needed you. Thank you for that, but now I must do what I need to do for myself."

"Dear, remember what I said about using your power. Please be careful."

"I will, I said."

I went to my place and packed up my stuff. I said my goodbyes in the morning, and when Ben showed up, I left to go to my new home at the ranch. My dog behaved well in the car, which was rear as rear can be. He is usually all over the place when I see him. I went to sleep on our way up to the ranch. Ben woke me up when we got there, and we went inside. His sister met us at the door, took our coats, and helped me up to my room with my luggage.

I unpacked my things, then met Ben and his sister Magie downstairs. I thanked her for letting me move up here to the ranch. It means so much to me.

"You are welcome; it will be nice to have someone to talk to besides the ranch hands."

I smiled and said, "Thank you," again. "This means so much to me." "This is my dog Peppi." Maggie rubbed my dog's head and said hi. He greeted her with a big, sloppy, wet kiss on her hand. She giggled and started to play with him.

Chapter 8

"I love dogs." She said.

"I am so glad to be here. I love being on the ranch, and I love being with all of you. I cannot wait to get to work. However, it will take some getting used to. I have not taken care of animals since I left Montana. I should be able to pick it back up again in no time." Ben walked me to my room and kissed me good night.

"Go to sleep, and do not worry about anything tonight."

"Good night, Ben."

"Good night, Lola."

I went into my room, showered, and then went to bed. The following morning, Ben took me to the stables, and we got the horses ready and went horseback riding. We went down by the clearing. By the time we were done riding for the day, it was late. We returned the horses to the stables and let the stable hands care for them. We had dinner and sat by the fireplace for a while. Then Ben walked me to my room.

"Good night, Lola; I must return to the city tomorrow morning. I will leave before you get up; I will call you when I arrive."

"Good night, Ben." I went into my room, took a shower, and then went to bed

When Ben returned to the city, I felt alone for the first time in a long time. Ben was not here to take me on sleigh rides, and I had to work. I had to muck out horse stalls and take care of the pigs. Ben called me that night and asked me how the day went. It went horribly because you were not here, and I had to do all the work myself today.

"I did not have a good dinner because I was tired, but I fed the dog and showered. As soon as I am done talking to you, I am going to bed. I cannot wait to see you again. I feel so lonely right now. I do not have my aunt to talk to anymore. I told her I would be there on the weekend, and we will do something while I am there."

"What would you like to do when I get back up there?"

"Well, if I can't go to see my aunt this weekend, I would like to go see a movie."

"Right now, though, I just want to sleep."

"Look up what is playing, and I will take you."

When I got to the ranch, I took Lola to dinner, and then we watched a movie. We sat in the back row, where I like to sit so no one could see us. I always enjoyed my time with her, no matter what we were doing. I hated to leave her, and I did not want to go back to the city anymore. I wanted to stay with her. I cannot wait to move up here so I can be here with her and be next to her all the time. It drives me crazy to be away from her this long.

"Lola, I am leaving for the city tomorrow morning. I have some things to take care of there, then I will be back up here for the week."

"I will miss you so much, though."

"I know, but" I will be up here more often because you are here now. I have been tying some things up down there because I will be moving up here permanently in a few months.

"Then I will only be going to LA occasionally to see how everything is going in the office. You are welcome to come with me on those occasions to see your friends and spend time with your aunt."

"Thank you. Just let me know ahead of time so I can make sure my aunt is around those days."

"Walk with me."

It was snowing and cold out, but I love walking in the snow. "

Okay, let me get my jacket."

"We will have to get you a warmer jacket since you will be here most of the time." When we were walking, I asked her if there was anything I could get her from the city.

"I can't think of anything right now."

"Okay," he said.

Her back was to me, so I made a snowball and threw it at her. She turned around and said, "You did not, and then make one and throw it at me."

And the snowball fight began.

We did not stop until we both were laughing and out of breath; I stood there trying to calm down. I threw my arms around his neck and kissed him.

He answered my kiss with a much harder one and lightly threw me to the ground. I could not move because he was on top of me. He kissed me again with more urgency this time.

"God, I am going to miss you," he said.

"I will miss you too."

"Let us return to the ranch before we freeze to death."

"Yes, let us go."

"I have to eat something and pack to get back to the city. I am leaving early; I will be gone before you wake up."

When we got to the house and opened the door, I smelled apple pie. We entered the kitchen, and I asked if I could have a piece of the pie.

"Of course, you can," Maggie said.

I took a piece and took a bite. The first thought that came to mind was my mother's cooking. Suddenly, my eyes started to tear up, and I put the pie down, apologized, and ran out of the room.

My sister looked at me, and I explained to her that Lola's parents had died in a car crash a few months ago. The pie must have triggered a memory. Ben found me in the living room.

"Are you okay?"

"I am better now. I hope your sister does not think bad of me."

"No, she does not; I told her the reason that may be behind the way you left the room."

"Thank God, I could not bear it if she did."

We ate something, and then Ben walked me to my room. He kissed me good night. The kiss was hard and hungry, like he could not get enough of me.

When he finally broke the kiss, I said good night, went into my room, and closed the door.

I left early; I needed to get everything done before I moved to the ranch. I have to do a promotion and find a new manager to manage my office. All the time that I have been here in the city, I have been thinking of Lola. I cannot get her out of my thoughts. I miss her so much. I cannot wait to see her again.

I would have moved already if I did not have much to do here in the city. I told my staff I was returning to the ranch on the weekend. I left the office early to clean my apartment and wash some clothes. I packed some fresh clothes in my suitcase and put it into my car. I wanted to leave the office, and I did not want to stop to pack before I went.

I put someone I could trust in the manager's position, and I am training him to do my job. Now, I have to find someone to fill his job. Everyone has off on the weekend, so I do not have to worry about being here for them, but that makes the weekend short. I will have to leave on Sunday to be there at the office on Monday. I will not be with Lola if I want to be this weekend.

Oh well, I thought to myself, it is only for a few months. Damn, a few months is going to feel like years. I cannot believe it is Friday already, I thought to myself. It will only be a few short hours, and I will go to the ranch again. I really cannot wait to see Lola again. I have been dreaming of her ever since I came back to the city.

I went to one of my favorite jewelry stores and bought Lola a necklace for her beautiful neck. I plan to take her out to dinner and give it to her then. I arrived at the ranch late, and everyone was sleeping, so I would have to wait until tomorrow to give it to her. I went to my room and went to bed.

I slept so well that I woke up late this morning, so everyone was outside attending to the animals, and I saw a note on the table that they cooked some breakfast for me. I have to warm it up. It was snowing out, so I quickly ate and went out to help them out. When we were done, we went into the house, ate some lunch, and took a nap. When we woke up, it was time to feed the animals again. After we were done for the day, I told Lola to take a shower and get something warm on. We are going out.

"Okay, where are we going to eat?"

"It is a surprise, he said."

We arrived at the restaurant and ordered our food. When we were done eating, he said, "I have another surprise for you," he slid a small red box over to me. I opened it and gasped.

"Do you like it? He asked."

"Yes, it is beautiful."

"Stand up and come over to me so I can put it on for you." He said. I went to him, and he told me to turn around with her back to him.

"Oh, Ben, I love it." She said with tears in her eyes.

"I am glad you like it.

"I have to go back to LA tomorrow. Thank God, I only have to do these trips for a few more months. I hate leaving you up here alone."

"I am not alone,"

"You know what I mean."

"Yes, I know what you mean," I smile. "It is only for a few months, I reminded him."

"I know, he said, but I do not like it."

"If I did not have to be in LA looking for someone to replace me, I would not be there." "I cannot wait until I am up here Permanently."

We are now done eating our food, and he paid the bill.

"Let us get home, he said. I have to leave early in the morning."

When we got back to the ranch, everyone was sitting by the fireplace, enjoying some hot chocolate and telling stories. I unfortunately couldn't join in on the fun because I had to get some sleep. I went straight to my room, packed my clothes, and then tried to get some sleep.

I had left before anyone was up this morning. I stopped for coffee before I left town, then went on my way to LA. When driving my car, I kept feeling like something was wrong. I could not put my finger on it, though. This feeling is disconcerting. My car is new and should not be acting up. The feeling was getting worse the closer I got to LA. I don't know if the feeling concerns my car or LA.

I got to LA late in the afternoon, so I just got something to eat and went to my apartment. I had to go to work tomorrow early in the morning. I have to start interviewing people for the open position.

When I was at work, an unexpected guest came to my office. It was my brother.

"What are you doing here,"

"I have not seen you for a while."

"Well, There's a reason for that. I think you should leave my office before I remove you."

"Look, I know we have our differences, but I am here to tell you that Shiloh is up to something." "I do not know what it is, but I do know it is not good." "I know she has been watching you and your girlfriend for a while now." "I just could not get the chance to get to see you." "She is always hanging around, and she has mentioned you two more than once, and no matter our feelings towards each other, I do not want anything to happen to you or your girlfriend."

"Also, I know she is working with someone, but I do not know who." "I will try snooping around to see if I can find anything for you, but it will not be easy." "Shiloh keeps that stuff concealed; she doesn't like to talk about it even with me. It is like she does not trust me."

"I wouldn't trust you either."

"I know, Ben," but please trust me on this. She is up to no good."

The next day, I spent time with Shiloh and tried to get information from her, but with no prevail. She does not trust me, and quite frankly, I would not trust me either. I have done some pretty shiny stuff in my life. I have to do something so she will trust me, but I don't know what and how to get her to trust me.

I am also trying to make good with my brother. I want to be a part of his life. I hope he lets me in after all these years, but that is unimportant. I have to figure out what Shiloh is up to. Damn it, I wish she would talk to me, but I know that is not going to happen. I will either have to hire an investigator or be one myself.

I know my brother and his girlfriend are in danger, but if I can't find any information, I won't be able to help them. Thank God, right now, Lola is up at the ranch. She will be safer there. My brother, on the other hand, is here in LA in the middle of the danger.

I followed Shiloh around to see if I could find anything to help me determine what she was up to. On the days that we spent time together, she always talked about how she loved the woods, so I thought that I would start there. She has been meeting someone there. I am sure of it.

One day, I followed Shiloh into the woods to where she was going. It turns out that she was meeting someone there, just like I thought. She has been meeting this person for a while because they are friends. Shiloh had never told me anything about this person. This person was dressed in a cloak that covered her face so I could see what they looked like. I do know that the person is a female just by the way she moved.

Shiloh, I don't know what they are up to, but I know it is not good, I think to myself.

I tried to get close enough to hear, but I couldn't because of all the brush beside me. I will have to talk to her about it someday soon to see if she will let me in on it. Just long enough to see what is going on.

What is she doing with this woman? It just doesn't make any sense to me. I left the sight, got back into my car, and drove back to the city. I was hoping to see my brother to let him know what I found out so far. Although it was not much, it was something. He has already left the office for the day, and I learned he goes away on the weekends.

Unfortunately, no one would tell me the address so I could find him; no one trusted me, and I hated that feeling. It is the worst feeling in the world.

I am going to set up something so I can talk to Shiloh. The more I spent time with her, the more she trusted me. I called her and asked her to go out with me. I told her that we could go anywhere she wanted to go. I thought one day she would take me to see the woman in the woods.

When we went out, I treated her like she was my girlfriend. She took the bait completely. I will never let on that I have another reason for wanting to be with her. If it comes to it in the future, then I will have to, but as of right now, I won't say anything.

I asked Shiloh what she had done that day, knowing she might not tell me. She just said I went to see my grandmother. Which I know was not true because I was there in the woods watching her. She is not a stupid girl by any means. It is going to be hard getting information out of her.

I will have to poke around to see if she knows anyone who might not be as tight with her as she thought. They would know something.

She would tell them because she thinks that they like her, and she has trust in them. I have seen her with some people so they could tell me something.

I asked Shiloh to go out with me again. We can get some dinner.

We can get a burger and hang out doing nothing if she wants. I have to remember what my goal is here. I am just trying to get information out of her. I need to see what she is up to so I can report to my brother. Right now, he is away and has no idea what is going on here.

I have no idea what is going on, either. Shiloh still won't open up to me because she does not trust me, and my brother will not talk to me for the same reason. I have to get her to trust me just enough for me to find the information I need. It bothers me that I don't know what she is planning. I keep asking around, but no one knows, or they don't want to get involved. I don't blame them one bit because Shiloh can be conniving.

I picked Shiloh up for our date, ordered a burger and fries, and sat outside at one of the tables. I was talking to her to see what she would say. I said that one of my favorite places was the wood, as she called it. I asked her if she knew any place here that I could go, and she said yes. I will take you someday; I have been meeting someone in a spot and would love you to meet her.

Wow, I can't believe she just offered up that information. I was expecting something else entirely. I thought that she would ask me why I wanted to know.

Okay, set it up with the person that you have been meeting with. I would love to meet the person that you have been meeting, but only if you are sure about it. I am okay with it. I will set it up the next time I see her. I will be seeing her tomorrow, and then I will let you know.

It is now the following day, and I meet my grandmother in the woods. I talked to her to see if she was up to meeting my friend. She said that it was okay to bring him.

"The more the merrier. If I decide that he fits our plans, then I will let him in on them."

"Wait, what plans?"

"You will see when we meet next."

"Okay, I will tell him you said it is okay for me to bring him."

I called Nick and told him everything was set up, and she said yes to meeting you.

"Cool, when are we going to meet?"

"We will meet the day after tomorrow in the afternoon."

"Cool, I can't wait; I love meeting new people," I told her, so she does not suspect anything.

Chapter 9

"I will see you then, she said."

I cannot wait to report something to my brother. I have been trying to help him ever since Shiloh started acting weird. I will see what I find out before I report back to Ben because whatever Shiloh is up to has more to do with my brother's girlfriend than with my brother himself.

I keep having this nagging feeling that something is not right. What is Shiloh's deal and obsession with Ben?

At least I will have something to go on after I meet whoever Shiloh is meeting with. I hope to find out something that I could tell Ben about. In two days, I will meet the person Shiloh has been meeting; I may eliminate this nagging feeling that something is wrong.

Meanwhile, Ben and his girlfriend are away for the weekend.

Shiloh has picked me up to meet the person she has been meeting in the woods. She took me deep inside the forest wooded area. The place was a clearing in the middle of the location. I say location because, to me, It did not look like an ordinary place. It looked like somewhere out of a fairy tale.

It was lush with greenery and surrounded by trees that looked to me could come alive at any time.

The woman came from what looked like a portal in the middle of the clearing. She had the same black cloak on the day I saw her.

Shiloh introduced us, "Grandmother, this is Nick, and Nick, this is my Grandmother Morgan." "She is the queen witch of the fairies."

"Shiloh, you did not tell me that she was your grandmother and the queen of the fairies."

"Are you bothered by it?'

"No, but you should have told me so I would have been shocked."

"Why are you so shocked? I asked him. I thought you knew."

"Why, did you think that I would know? I ask her."

"Well, I thought you knew because I have pointy ears and other things of the fay. I never thought of it because I never judge anyone by their appearance."

"Okay, so what am I seeing here? I have never seen anything like this in my life."

"Well, my grandmother is a witch who lives in a world that most people in the mundane world can't see."

"Okay, why can I see it then?"

"You can see it because you believe you can, so it is not hidden.

"It is nice to meet you, ma'am. I said."

"Hello Nick, it is nice to meet you too. You can call Queen Morgan."

"Shiloh, do you deem him trustworthy? My grandmother asks me."

"yes."

"Good, do you know what happens if I find out differently? Don't you?"

"Yes, grandmother."

"Well, let us see if he can take some pain, shall we?" I pulled out my staff and gave him a little jolt of lighting, and zapped him good.

"Ouch, for what did you do then?"

"I did it to ensure you know what will happen if you betray me. It will be a lot worse if you do. I will not tolerate someone who is disobedient. Do you understand me, Nick?"

"Yes, Queen Morgan.

"Now, back to this matter. Shiloh, did you get the information that I sent you to get?"

"Yes, grandmother, Ben, and his girlfriend go up north to the family ranch on the weekend. Lola has moved up there because I heard her give her notice at work. I have not seen her here in LA for a while now."

"Well, we will have to pay my sister-in-law a little visit. Did you find out where she is living?"

"Yes, I did, grandmother. She lives not too far from here in LA."

"Okay, let us go. All of us are going, even your dear Nick. I want him to see what happens when you are not doing as you should."

"I look at Nick and shrug my shoulders."

"This is some scary shit," I said to Shiloh.

"What? It's too late to back out now, Nick."

I didn't think you were going to drag me into your shit."

"To tell you the truth, Nick. I just found out that she had plans on bringing you into this. I just thought that she wanted to meet you. Let us get this over with. I do not want to hurt anyone."

We were now at my sister-in-law's house. I do not even knock. I barge in.

"Well, well, well, sister, what do we have here."

I am sitting in my kitchen, and I hear the witch barge into my house.

"What did I do to deserve you coming here?"

"It is not what you did; it is what you will do."

"Okay, I will bite; what will I tell you?"

"You are going to tell me Lola is."

"I would rather die first."

"That you will do if you do not tell me what I want to know."

"I will die anyway, so I do not care."

"You may, but it is up to you on how you die. You know I like a toy occasionally. If you do not tell me what I want to know, I will kill you, but not before I toy with you first."

Do what you will. I am not going to tell you."

"I do not know why you are so loyal to that brat."

"I am loyal to her because she did not ask to be brought into this world."

"Shiloh, Nick, tie my dear sister-in-law to a chair and make sure she does not get free."

"Nick, I know you do not want to do this, but we have no choice now." I did as I was told only because I feared for my life.

"I warned you, sister, now you will die."

"Oh, dear sister, you should have told me what I want to know.

"Why are you going to kill me anyway?

"That's true, but if you told me, I would have killed you fast. Now, I am going to do it slowly. I will start from your feet and work my way up to your head until you die."

I start with incredibly low-intensity voltage and at her feet. I intensify the electricity every time I give her another jolt.

"You know that I love to play with my pray. Are you going to give me the information or not?"

"No, I said as I spat at her."

"Okay, here is another jolt for you, and I gave her another zap of electricity." "That one is for telling me no, and this one is for spitting at." I gave another zap. "You know, I can sit here all day and do this."

"Shiloh, why is she doing this? She already knows the information."

"She is doing it because she wants to. She can be ruthless at times." She said with tears in her eyes.

"Are you ready to talk my sister?"

"No, I will never betray Lola. I do not care what you do to me."

"Well, I will tell you my little secret; I already know the information I want. I am just doing this for my entertainment."

Then my grandmother gave her one last jolt, and she was dead, then my grandmother, Nick, and I left.

"My dear, Shiloh, I must go home for the night, but I will be back in two weeks, and we will go to this ranch that Lola is at."

"Okay, grandmother."

"In the meantime, have a good time doing whatever you do." Then, she was gone in a flash of smoke.

"Shiloh, I cannot believe what I just saw. She killed that woman just because she wanted to."

Yes, I know, and unfortunately, it was Lola's aunt. She had killed her parents also by causing them to get into a car crash. You see, Lola's mother was from the fay world and came here to the mundane world to go to school and meet someone and fell in love. They married and had Lola."

"Lola's mother was thought a trader by her people and excommunicated; after that, they were hunted and eventually found and killed.

That is why Lola was here in LA. She had moved here after her parents died. Now, Morgan, my grandmother is hunting Lola to kill her and anyone that gets in her way."

"Well, she said she would be back in two weeks. I hope that is enough time to warn them."

"Nick, so that you know, I had no idea what she had planned today. She does not always tell me everything."

"Ah, that is why you have not mentioned her or this before."

"Yes,"

"Okay, right now, Ben is at the ranch. He is there for the weekend. I believe he will be back at his office. I will talk to him then. In the meantime, what do we do?"

"I don't know; we just have to wait to see what happens next."

"I have never experienced anything like this. I mean, I used to do some shitty stuff, but nothing compared to this. I do not have the stomach for this shit."

Now it is Monday, and I have to tell my brother Ben what has happened. God, I am deciding to go to see my brother.

I called my brother and asked if I could see him.

"Yes, you can come in half an hour. Just give me time to settle in."

"Okay, I have some news about what is going on." I am sitting in his office and trying to figure out how to tell him what it has to do.

"There is no uncomplicated way to say this," I told him.

"Just give it to me, I said to him."

"Please keep in mind I had to be involved to make it look like I was there to be involved. I told him. Oh boy, here goes."

"One day, I was following Shiloh and watching what she was doing. I followed her to a wooded area, and I saw her talking to someone there. I could not see anything other than that, so I left. I asked Shiloh out on a date so I could go undercover. She had no idea what I had on my mind, so she said yes."

"We went out for burgers and fries. The next thing I knew, I was meeting the person she had been meeting.

On the meeting day, she said that the person was her grandmother. It turns out that her grandmother is Morgan, Queen of the fay witches. I came here to warn you about what she is up to."

"This woman is pure evil. It makes me sick to even think of what she has done. I have done some shitty stuff in my life, but this woman takes the cake over me. Morgan killed Lola's aunt."

"Holy shit, when, how, where?"

"Remember, I was there only because I was undercover and kept an open mind about what I was about to tell you. I had to make everything look real, or she would have killed me on the spot. Last weekend, when you were gone, we went to her house, and Morgan was looking for information she already had."

"Like I said, this woman is nothing but pure evil. She torched Lola's aunt by zapping her with the electricity from her staff. In the end, when she was about to die, Morgan told her that she already had the information she needed. She killed her because she would not betray Lola. You and Lola are not safe. It would be best if you went somewhere other than the ranch. Morgan knows where Lola is, and she will kill her and anyone who gets in the way."

I am involved because I was stupid to think that everything was going to go as I planned. She will kill me when she finds out that I betrayed her.

"She will torture me first like she did Lola's aunt."

"Did you say, Morgan?"

"Yes, why?"

"Because she's Lola's grandmother too, and she killed Lola's parents and now her aunt."

"Shiloh just told me that Morgan was her grandmother. She also told me about Lola and Morgan being her grandmother, too."

"I will call our sister to let her know what is happening."

"Speaking of our sister. How is she doing?"

"She's doing good."

I called my sister and told her the situation. I asked her not to tell Lola and that I would tell her when I got up there.

"I am coming right away and bringing Nick with me." I could tell that my sister didn't like that I was bringing Nick, but I told her right now, I have no choice.

I told my staff that I had to go to a family emergency and asked them to take care of things here. I will explain everything later. They all were okay with it. Then Nick and I left to get packed. I stayed with him at his place to make sure he was safe. Then we went to my place so I could pack, and off we went.

We made it up to the ranch in no time, but it was late when we reached the ranch, so I quietly took Nick to one of the spare rooms and then went to my room. We had to wait until morning to tell everyone what was going on.

It was morning, and I talked with everyone on hand so my sister Maggie could relay the information to the others. We need everyone's cooperation. Keep from telling anyone where we are going.

I told Lola to get packed, and we must go somewhere else. "I have other places that we could go to. The home is furnished, so pack your clothes. Oh, leave your dog here; he will be safe here for the time being. Maggie will bring him when she comes to our new place."

"Okay," I said.

She packed everything she could think of, and we went to our new place. When we were in the car, I told Lola and Nick I had a place up north near San Francisco. "We are going there for a while."

"Lola," I said. I have some unwelcome news. I wanted to wait until we were alone. Well, as alone as we can be anyway. But first, this is my brother Nick. I do not know how to tell you this."

"It is about my aunt, isn't it?"

"Yes."

"She is dead, isn't she?"

"Yes."

"Wait, how did you know? Nick asked."

"I have special powers. I have the gift of healing and just discovered that I have the gift of psychic sight."

"What do you mean? Nick asked."

'I mean, my mother was from the Fay world, and my father was from the mundane world. I am part Fay."

"No wonder Morgan is after you."

Did you say Morgan? I asked him.

"Yes, why? He asked."

"She is my grandmother and killed my parents," I told him.

"Oh wow, Shiloh told me she was also her grandmother," Nick said.

"Holly Shit. I said. I feel like I do not know who I am anymore. I wonder how much my aunt knew about my parents. I will never know, will I? I said. I had a feeling that something was coming."

"You are not scared?" Nick asked.

"Yes, I am scared shitless, but I cannot let that get in the way. She thinks of me as tainted blood. My aunt warned me about using my power because Morgan would hunt me down. I am not afraid of using my power. Eventually, I will have to use them on someone that gets hurt. I swear the woman is butt-hurt over her daughter marrying a man from the mundane world. She needs to get over it."

"Aren't you sad and want to cry over your aunt's death?"

"I have my way of mourning."

After we arrived at my other place up north, Nick approached me and asked me if I were afraid that when Morgan got to the ranch, she would kill the rest of the people there.

"I know she will try; that is why I told everyone left to go in different directions."

"Let us get settled," I want to check in on Lola. She has not said too much since we told her about her aunt. I am worried about her. She has not even shown signs of mourning the loss of her, and that is not a good sign."

"Lola, are you okay?" Ben asked.

"No, she replied. Everything has turned to shit."

I took Lola to our room and showed her where the bathroom was in case she wanted to take a bath.

"A bath sounds good right about now. I think I will take one."

"Take your time. I will be in to dry you off."

"Okay, I will wait for you then."

"I am going to talk to Nick for a while."

I went into the living room to talk to Nick. I asked him if there was anything else that I needed to know.

"No, that is all the information that I have. Oh, Morgan said that she was going to see Shiloh again in two weeks. If that is anything useful to you."

"It is, I said. I will go down and check on things in LA about that time. Can you keep your eyes on Lola and take care of her?"

'I am not going anywhere, so yes.'

"I will only be gone for a couple of days."

"I do not want to leave Lola alone, but I must check up on things there. There is no way around it. Just as I was saying it, my phone rang. I picked it up, and it was one of my staff. They told me that one of the staff was killed."

"Okay, get round-the-clock security. I will be there in a couple of days. I hung up the phone."

"Shit, now she is after my staff. I have to go now. I will talk to you later. Right now, I have to tend to Lola."

"Lola, are you done?"

"Yes, you can come in." She said. I started to dry her off.

"I just got some more unwelcome news. One of my staff was killed. I must go to LA. While I am gone, Nick will be here to keep you company."

"Do you think Morgan did it?" I asked him,

"I don't know," I said. I will know something more once I get down there.

"I hope everything is okay there. Did you call Maggie to let her know we got here, okay?"

No, I was about to when someone called me from the office. I will call her when you are getting dressed for bed. I will be right back. I went to get my phone. It was still in the living room. I called my sister and told her we arrived at my place okay. "Did the others go to other places?" I asked her.

"Yes, everyone went their separate ways." She said.

"Good, at least I do not have to worry about that. I said. I just got a phone call that one of my staff was killed."

"Oh no, do you think Morgan did it?"

"I don't know, and I will not know until I get down there. Right now, that is the only lead I have." I said goodbye to Maggie and hung up the phone.

I went back to the bedroom, and Lola was crying.

"I know it hurts, and I know it is so soon after your parents' death. Do you feel comfortable enough with me for me to stay with you tonight?"

"Yes, I told him. I have been comfortable for a while now."

"I know, I said; I just wanted to make sure. I am so sorry that I have to go down to LA. I do want to leave you alone. My brother will be here, but it is not like me being here. Especially now. I do not want to leave you in your time of need."

Go, I said to him. I know you have to do this. The death of one of your employees was unexpected, and you have to take care of things there, too."

"Yes, it is unfortunate that it happened. I have to go and investigate. I am only going to go down there for a couple of days. I will let you know if I have to stay longer."

Okay, I said. For now, let us get some sleep.

I need to leave in a couple of days, so I spent most of my time with Lola. When we went to bed, I just laid by her side and let her snuggle up to me; I knew this was not the time to push her sexually. I spent all my time devoted to everything she wanted and needed.

Chapter 10

The time went fast, so I had to leave for LA.

I am going to miss you. Lola said.

"I know, I will not be staying for that long. I do not want to leave you for that long in your time of need."

I packed some clothes and put them in the trunk of my car so I did not have to do it in the morning. I woke up before Lola this morning. I grabbed a cup of coffee and woke Lola up to say goodbye. I will call you when I get down there.

"Okay, be safe," I said.

"I will," I told her. I am not even gone yet, and I cannot wait to be back. I kissed her on the cheek and said bye, then left. When I was driving my car, I had that uneasy feeling again. Something is not right. The closer I got to LA, the more I felt uncomfortable. I could not get a handle on it.

When I got to the office, everything and everyone was in uproar. I faced confusion like I never had before. My office, which was usually neat, was messy. The people looked at me to fix the situation. I was on the verge of pulling my hair out because of all the chaos. But life had to go on.

I have someone investigating who murdered one of my staff. Although I have a feeling who it was. I have to make sure. If it were who it was, the only one who could help was Lola, and I do not want to put her in the middle of this. How can I fix this if I cannot fight it?

Lola is the only one who has magical powers and can fight them in the magical world.

The investigator returned with something, and thank God, it was not what I thought. The person from the office that was murdered was not murdered by who I thought he was. He was done in by someone that he had made angry. Not to sound harsh, but at least I do not have to pull Lola into this mess.

Now, I must go to the funeral and return to San Francisco. I don't want to leave Lola and my brother alone too long. God knows what can go wrong. I don't feel right about this whole thing; being here without Lola is wrong.

I went to my apartment, ordered some food, got everything ready for tomorrow's funeral, and went to bed. I did not get that much sleep, though, because of the uneasy feeling I have had since I got here in LA.

I know somehow Morgan Is behind this, and I cannot prove it. I just have this feeling that she is.

When I return north, I must ask Lola if she can sense anything. The only thing is if she uses her power, then Morgan will sense her. I don't particularly appreciate that I have to involve Lola at all. Still, she is the only one that can help.

Her aunt had warned her what would happen if she used her powers. Lola was told that if she used her powers, Morgan would sense her and hunt her down, and I do not want that to happen, but what choice do I have?

I feel torn between what I must and do not want to do. Right now, I have to go to this funeral and do my due diligence. When I am done here, I will leave town for a while.

I had my clothes packed and in my car, so I did not have to stop back at my place before I was to leave. I am back on the road to go up north now. I cannot wait to see Lola and my brother. I thought I would never say I cannot wait to see him, but it is true. Most of all, I cannot wait to see Lola.

I still cannot get this driving feeling that something is wrong. I called Lola, and she said everything is good up there, but something is nagging at me.

It could be that because everything is happening all at one time. Currently, I don't know what is bothering me.

Right now, I cannot wait to see Lola. I was halfway up north, and I had to pull over and stop the car because I felt physically sick. I had to take a break from driving, which slowed me down.

I have to keep my head on straight; this feeling isn't letting me do that. I really must talk to Lola about this. She is the only one who can help me with this, I am afraid. I called her again and told her what was happening to me.

"I will see what I can do. I told him. You know I am not supposed to use my powers, but I will do it for you." I told him.

"I know, he said, and I appreciate what you must do."

"If Morgan is somehow involved in the feelings you're having, I will have to do something."

"I know that too," I said to her. I will let you go so you can do what you must do. I will be there in a little while."

"Okay," she said.

I let Nick know that I was going to my room to meditate because Ben wasn't feeling well and couldn't get the feeling that something was wrong out of his head.

"Okay," he said.

I go to my room for privacy and set up for my meditation to see what messages I can see. I set my candles around me in a circle of protection and light them. I also draw out the circle with my finger. I begin the meditation with a prayer, then let the quietness and stillness settle over me.

The first thing I get is Morgan is hunting me, which I already knew. There is someone with her, though. It might be Shiloh, but I am not sure. I know that the person with her is a small woman. That much, I know.

How is Morgan involved in Ben's feelings? I asked. I got something right away. I got that she was trying to prevent him from getting to me. Somehow, she has figured out where I am. Now, I know that she will come here. If I have to face her, I must.

I called Ben back. I told him she knows where we were and was trying to prevent him from getting here. "Just please focus and get back here safely," I said.

"I will, he said. And hung up the phone."

I got back on the road more focused than ever and wanted to get to Lola before it was too late. Lola could manage just about anything, but I wonder if she could manage Morgan alone.

I need to be there to help Lola if she needs it.

Also, I need to find out how much help Nick would be. He has bent to Morgan's will before, and I am not sure if he will not again.

Morgan can make the strongest person bent to her will. Lola must fight Morgan's power over her if she wants to survive.

I am worried about her now that she has told me Morgan knows where she is. I know Morgan can kill Lola if she has the chance.

I have to get there. I cannot let anything bother me while I am on the road. Now I am speeding to get to Lola and Nick. More Lola that Nick right now needs me. Lola's in more danger than Nick. Morgan wants to kill Lola because she is a so-called tainted blood. So, her aunt told her.

Being half-human is her downfall. Unfortunately, it is Morgan's downfall also. I know Lola's heart. She will never let Morgan overcome her if she can.

I got to my place just in time. Morgan was right behind me. I got out of the car and ran into the house. I tell Lola that Morgan is here and will not take No for an answer. She is ready to fight, and she has Shiloh with her.

"I knew she had someone with her, and I thought it might be Shiloh, but I was not sure. I told Ben. Nick has told me that Shiloh sometimes does not know what Morgan is planning, and I believe it. Shiloh is not that cold-hearted. She might be on the evil side, but somehow, it is more because of Morgan than anything else."

"I am trying to give Shiloh the benefit of the doubt. I do like her."

"I know you did, but right now, we must focus on the problem," I told her.

"I know, she said. Let us try not to harm her, please. I can heal her if she does get hurt, but I do not know if I can do anything if she dies."

"Okay," we said.

"She is here, I said. I can hear her calling my name. Wow, she is pissed."

Morgan isn't one for beating around the bush. She wants to talk to me, and she will not take no for an answer. I went out the door and faced her with all the courage I could muster. I don't know how to use my power yet, so I plan to avoid conflict. She is acting like that won't be the case, though.

"Lola, I have come for you," Morgan said.

What are you doing here, Morgan?" "I have not done anything for you even to come to seek me out."

"You know why I am here." She said.

"I know, I said, and I also know that you are my grandmother."

Shiloh looked at Morgan and said, "You did not tell me that Lola was related to me."

"I did not see any reason to mention it," Morgan said.

"Are you telling me that I am going to fight a person that is related to me?"

Shiloh suddenly got this look in her eyes and said, NO. Then started to come over to us. But before she could get to us, Morgan struck her down with her staff.

"Morgan, if you know what's good for you, you better get off my property before I make you leave."

"I will be back, Morgan said. And I will not be alone."

I went to Shiloh and put my hands above her chest, and a big ball of light emerged. "I hope this works. I have never healed anyone before." In a minute or two, Shiloh came to.

"Thank you, Shiloh said. I swear, I did not know you were related to me."

"That is okay, I said to her. Nick told me that Morgan does not tell you everything."

"Now, we must find out how we are related."

"Can I please stay here with you? I do not feel safe now."

"Yes," I told her. "But somehow, we must contact your parents to let them know you are safe."

Shiloh began to cry.

"Shiloh, what's wrong?"

"Morgan killed my parents," she told me when she picked me up to come here."

"Oh, Shiloh, I am so sorry."

"Since a wooded area surrounds you, I can poke around to see if any of the Fae know how we are related."

"Just be careful doing it. Morgan probably has everyone that is with her looking for us."

"I will, she said."

"For now, I need to rest."

I showed Shiloh to her room and then left her to rest. I went back out to talk to Ben and Nick about what we could do about Morgan.

"What are we going to do about Morgan?" I asked.

"I don't know, they both said. I know that we have to do something, though. She has caused enough pain already."

"Let us start with what we already know."

"We know that she is coming back, and she is bringing back up. We also know that she loves playing with her victims. Her magic seems to come from her staff."

"Maybe if we can somehow take it from her, we can beat her at her own game."

"When Shiloh wakes up, I will see if she knows anything to help us defeat her." Shiloh slept all night after her ordeal with Morgan. "Poor girl had no idea that she was related to me in any way. I did not know either."

"It surprised the hell out of me too. Ben said. I had no idea. That means when I was dating her, Morgan was behind everything she had done to me."

"Now, we must figure out how she is related to me. If she is my sister, that means that one of my parents was unfaithful. If she is my niece, then that means that one of my parent's sister or brother went with Fae also."

Wow, this is blowing my mind. Nick said.

When Shiloh woke up, we started to ask her questions about everything and anything she could tell us. She told us what we already knew. There was not anything new that she said. She also said that she would go into the woods and try to contact other Fae so she could try to get some information.

"You are not going anywhere for the next few days. I told her. You have to heal completely." I said.

"I know," she said. I do not want to do anything right now anyway. When I am feeling better in a few days, I will go.

I know you will protest what I say, but I must do this alone. The Fae are very private and do not like humans hanging around.

Shiloh, I am going with you. Lola said. I will stay back, but it is unsafe for you to go alone.

I could tell that Shiloh was thinking about it.

Chapter 11

I will not take NO for an answer. Do you understand me?

Yes, she finally said.

Now that you are here with us, it is up to us to make sure you are safe. In the meantime, get as much rest as possible, and do not worry about anything.

"I am hungry, Shiloh said. What is for dinner?

For you soup. I told her. It would be best to regain your strength before going into the woods and find any information you need.

Okay, she said.

Right after dinner, we should all go to bed and get some rest. I said. After we ate, everyone went to their rooms to rest. Ben took us to our room. I knew someday we would be alone, but I did not think it would be this soon. He said as I was sitting on the bed.

Do you trust me? He asked.

Yes, I said.

"Then lay on the bed. I want to do something. Know that I will not do anything that you do not want to do. If it gets too much, tell me, and I will stop."

"Okay," she said. And did what he asked.

"Don't move; if you do, I will tie you to the bed. Do you understand me, Lola?"

I took out my riding crop and showed it to her, and told her not to fear it. This will not hurt when I strike you with it, and to prove it, I lightly tapped her on the foot.

Did it hurt? I asked.

No, she said.

The way that I am going to use it will not hurt you anyway. I told her not to move, and I moved the riding crop up and down her body. I want to tease every part of your body. I told her. I trailed the riding crop everywhere. I started at her neck, then went further down to her breast and teased her nipples.

I gave her nipples a tap.

As I watched Lola come alive, I asked her if she liked what I was doing to her. She moaned, and I knew she wanted it, and I pushed forward.

I trailed it down to her stomach, and she moaned even louder. I started to go to the thighs, and she almost jumped off the bed. Then I tapped her clit, and she nearly came on the spot.

Not yet, Lola, I heard him say. I want to taste you as you come. I am going to put my mouth on you now. She was so turned on that when I put my mouth on her, she came hard.

I went back up so I could see her face. "I love the way you taste, Lola, and how you respond to me and what I do to you."

"Let's get some sleep," I said to her.

"I needed that; I told him. I was so wound up from all the events of the day."

"I know; that is one of the reasons I did what I did. Now, let us get some rest."

A couple of days passed, and Shiloh was getting better by the day.

"I feel so much better," Shiloh said.

I know; give it a couple of days more. I told her.

"I will," she said; once I can go into the woods and try to find the portal to the other world. Every wooded area has one. She explained. It may take some time. They are hidden for a reason. They do not like to mingle with the mundane world."

"What is for dinner? She asked. Please do not tell me more soup. I am so tired of it now."

"I know," Lola said. We will be out of the soup by tomorrow. One more night will not hurt you, will it?"

"No, I guess not." She said.

A couple of days went by, and Shiloh told us that she was ready to find the portal. I agreed that it was time to find it. We went into the woods, and I stayed back a wase and watched from afar as I told her I would do.

As I watched from where I was, I saw her sifting through the woods like someone on fire. She wants to find the portal as much as we all did. Unfortunately, she did not find it today.

"I am sorry I did not find anything today," Shiloh said.

"That okay, I said. We can look again tomorrow. I told her. Anyway, you did say that it might take some time to find it."

"I know, but I wanted to find it today. I am just as curious about how I am related to you."

Let us rest for the rest of the night. Lola said.

"Lola, why are you so nice to me after everything I did in LA and here?"

I always liked you, Shiloh, and I do not hold you accountable for what you did because you were manipulated into doing something that you had no idea of; that is why.

"It is still no excuse for the way I behaved."

"Do not worry about it," I said. We are all in this together now, and together we will win. We went back to the house.

"Do you like hot chocolate? I asked her."

"Oh yes, she said. Please, that sounds so nice right now. I am cold, and it will warm me up."

We sat in the living room drinking our hot chocolate, and suddenly, Ben came racing out of our room, yelling I must go to LA again; another one of my staff was killed.

Shiloh looked at me with wild eyes.

"Ben, Lola said. Shiloh is remembered here, and she is still recovering from our ordeal. Plus, she has never heard you yelling. You might frighten her."

"I am sorry, Shiloh." He said.

"I was a little frightened, but I understand why you are upset. You do not have to apologize for being upset."

"Oh, I forgot to ask if you found anything today." He said.

"Unfraternally, no, we did not. There is tomorrow, though." Shiloh said.

"Yes," Ben said.

"Now, if you will excuse me, ladies, I must go and pack so I can leave."

"Ben, I do not feel right about this trip. I can't get the feeling something isn't quite right. I do not know what it is, but I know something is wrong. Why don't you take Nick with you? We will be okay until you get back."

"Are you sure, Ben asked. I do not want to leave you two up here alone."

"Yes, we will be fine. Anyway, Shiloh and I have a lot to talk about and to get to know each other."

"Okay, he said. Nick, go pack your bags. You are coming to LA with me. Another one of my staff was killed. We said goodbye to the girls, and we went on our way down to LA".

"What is going on?" Nick asked.

"I did not want to say anything in front of Shiloh, but I got word that one of my staff was killed by Morgan."

"How do you know that it was Morgan?"

"Well, for one thing, she left a note that she is coming after us on the body."

"Fuck, she is going to go after anyone that gets in the way of her taking Lola down. That is the only thing she told us when we were at Lola's aunt's house. This all sucks, Nick said."

"Well, unfortunately, we cannot do anything about it until Shiloh discovers some information."

"Yeah, I know," Nick said.

Nick fell asleep, leaving me pondering my thoughts as I drove. I do not understand any of this anymore. Meanwhile, Lola and Shiloh are alone at the house, and I do not like that.

Chapter 12

Shiloh and I were drinking some hot chocolate and talking.

"Where did you grow up?" I asked.

"I grew up in LA, and I was adopted because my parents were killed in a plane crash."

"I am sorry. Lola said."

"Did you get to finish school?"

"Yes, I graduated high school. After that is when I met Morgan."

"I see," I said. She told you she was your grandmother and did not give you more information than that."

"Yes, that is it."

"I am so sorry that this happened to you, Shiloh."

"Initially, I thought she was nice, but when I did not do what she wanted, she would punish me. I wanted to get out, but by the time I realized what was going on, it was too late."

"Oh my god, I just realized that you said that your real parents were killed in a plane crash. My parents were killed in a car crash. I wonder if the accidents were related."

"Makes you wonder. Shiloh said. Well, anyway, that is the bulk of my story."

"My story is like yours. I grew up in Montana on a farm, though. I am not from the city. I am a small-town girl who wants to be happy. Unfortunately, my happiness did not last long. When I turned twenty-five, I sprouted pointed ears, and when I looked to my aunt for information, she told me that my mother was from the Fae world and my father was from the mundane world, and that's it at that time." She told me that I was a halfling."

"You are lucky; at least you had someone to look to. I did not. Shiloh said. When My powers started showing up, I had no one to help me through those times. Yes, I have powers. I have the power of sight and blowing shit up."

"Right now, I have the power of sight and healing. Lola said. I do not know if I have any other powers."

"Diddo," Shiloh said.

"I want to return to the woods when Ben and Nick return. I do not think it is safe. We can spend time together."

"I am happy that I found you. Shiloh said. Even if it was not the best way to find someone."

"I am happy you found me too. Lola said."

It was not too long, and Ben was calling me. "We made it down okay." He said.

"Good," I said.

"Everything here is in chaos. Ben said. I will be here for about five days to straight things out and go to the furfural."

"Okay, I said. Be careful, okay."

"I will," he said. Now, I must go. This place is such a mess."

He hung up the phone.

"That was Ben," I said. He said it is a mess there, and it will take them about a week to straighten everything out."

"Well, at least we have each other for company," Shiloh said.

"Yes, I agree. It is fun hanging out with you." I told her.

"Let's go outside and sit on the porch. I said. I will make us some tea to keep us warm." When the tea was done, we took it out on the porch with us and drank and chatted.

"I love the winter," Shiloh said.

"Me too, Lola said. I love the way everything looks when it snows. Everything is white and pretty."

"Yes, you do not see that in LA. I want to stay here forever." Shiloh said.

"All of us can stay here if everything goes okay. I want to stay here. It could be our new home. For now, let us be grateful we have a place to live. So, tell me about Nick."

"Nick came into my life totally by accident.

Shiloh said. After the fact, he told me he was sniffing around for his brother to see what I was up to because suspicious things were happening. We just hit it off. I wish it were not how it happened. He was tailing me because he saw me going into a wooded area like the one here. He unfortunately got involved in this whole mess. Now, he is hunted like the rest of us."

"This is very unfortunate. Lola said. Well, we have a whole five days to become friends. You are going to have to learn to dress simple."

"Why," Shiloh asked.

"Because I only have simple clothes, and we are about the same size," I said.

"I do not like it, but okay," Shiloh said with a frown.

I gave her some clothes, and she took them and put them in her room. I know that she is not happy about wearing clothes that do not fit her style, but that is what I have at the moment.

I made something for dinner, and we sat and watched a movie as we ate. By the time the movie was done, it was time to go to bed. We cleaned up our mess and headed to our rooms. Before that, I asked her if she liked to read.

"She said yes," so I gave her one of my books to read.

"We can be reading friends." She said.

"Yes," I told her.

She took the book gladly and went into her room. It was morning when Ben called me again.

"How is everything up there?" He asked.

"Quiet," I said, how I like it.

"Just be careful." He said.

"I will," I told him.

"We will be back by Saturday afternoon."

"Okay," I will be here.

"I hope so," He said and chuckled.

"How is Shiloh?" He asked.

"She is doing better," I said.

"Okay, I have to go by for now. He said. I will call you tomorrow."

"By, I said and hung up the phone.

When Shiloh finally came out of her room, it was nearly noon.

"What time did you go to sleep?"

"It was about one in the morning." She said. "The book you gave me was so good I did not want to put it down."

"I am glad you enjoyed it," I said. "I have plenty of books that you can read."

"Okay," she said. I only have a little of this book left. I will give it back to you when I am done. She said. Do you have any mysteries?"

"I will have to look," I said.

"In the meantime, I will make us some breakfast. I am having tea and toast. What do you want?"

"Tea and toast are fine." She said.

I made us both something to eat and then went to the porch. When we were done eating, I cleaned up and went to find Shiloh some books to read. I did find some mysteries that she wanted. I gave her them and said that they were all of them that I have.

"This is good," she said.

She went off to her room to read. I am so glad we found each other, even though it was not a good start to our relationship. It is off to a good start now. I am so happy for all the people that are in my life now. Well, all but one, Morgan. If it were not for Morgan, I would not have met Nick or Shiloh. Everything and everyone had their reason.

If I had not had to move to California, I would not have met Ben either. I am happy currently in my life. The only thing I am not pleased about is that I must fight Morgan. She has been a thorn in my side, and I will be glad to get rid of her.

Ben called and asked how we were doing.

"We are good," I said. I cannot wait to see you."

"Me too," I told her. Be ready for me, Lola. I am missing you, and Now I want to fuck you so hard you scream my name."

"You know, every time you say that, I get chills all over my body."

"Good, I love you, Lola. I would do anything for you. How's Shiloh?" I asked.

"She is good," I said. I gave her some books to read and some of my clothes because she had none. She did not like that she had to dress simple at first, but she is getting used to it."

"Nick is missing her."

"I will let her know.

"We will be home tomorrow." He said.

"I cannot wait to see you," I said. Oh, and Ben, I love you too."

"Okay, I will see you sometime tomorrow. Tell Shiloh that Nick will be back tomorrow."

"I will," I said and hung up the phone.

"Shiloh," I called out.

"Yes," she said.

"Ben asked me to tell you that Nick is coming back tomorrow."

"Okay. Thank you. I miss him so much." "I did not think I would feel like this about anyone."

"I know I felt the same way when I met Ben. I was always questioning myself about why he picked to be with."

"Let's get some rest tonight," I said. "They will be back sometime tomorrow."

"Okay, I was heading to bed when you called me."

"Good night," Shiloh said.

"Good night," Lola said.

I woke up first; I have been letting Shiloh sleep in because she has been going to bed late. After all, she has been reading late into the night. I made myself some breakfast and sat down to eat. When Shiloh finally woke up, it was in the afternoon. I asked her if she wanted something to eat.

"Yes, please."

I cooked her something, and we went out on the porch to enjoy what was left of the afternoon.

"Have you heard from the guys yet?" She asked.

"Yes, I said. They should be here in a couple of hours."

"Good," she said. I can't wait to see them and know they are safe. I also cannot wait to get back into the woods to see if I can find that damn portal and we can get the information we need."

"I know," I said. I want to know everything that there is to know. I also need to know how to defeat Morgan. We can go out tomorrow morning."

The guys got home shortly after we went inside for the night. The nights have been getting colder. I made everyone some hot chocolate, and we sat by the fireplace and discussed what happened in LA.

Ben and Nick told us that they think Morgan has something to do with the murders, but they have no proof. Shiloh said that she never leaves anything behind. No one can connect her to the murders then.

I really cannot believe any of this, but I do because you cannot make this shit up.

"We need to eat something. Is there anything in the fridge?" They said.

"Sure," Lola said. "What do you want?"

"Anything at this point would be fine," Ben said.

I cooked them something, and they ate quietly.

Ben was the first to talk. "I need some sleep," he said." Let's go, Lola; I want you in my bed sleeping beside me."

"Good night, Shiloh and Nick." Ben and I went to our room.

"Sorry, Lola, it is just sleep I want tonight."

"I have had a pretty shitty week. Tomorrow is another day for what I want to do to you."

I slipped under the blankets, and he snuggled next to me, and we went to sleep. In the morning, when everyone woke up, we ate breakfast and then went out on the porch for a while. We had nothing else to do, so we sat outside for quite a bit.

When it was time, we went into the house, had some lunch, and then cleaned up after we ate. Nick was with Shiloh, and Ben was with me, and we sat and talked. I told Ben that Shiloh and I had not been back into the woods since they had gone because I did not think it was safe.

"I did not expect you to go without us here anyway," Ben said. "I did not want you to go anyway; I just did not have time to talk to you about it before we left. I was in a hurry to get down to LA."

"I know," she said.

Shiloh missed Nick. She told me she never thought she would feel this way about anyone. And I told her I felt that way when I met you. I was always quietly asking myself why I would pick someone like me. I am not gorgeous, and I have nothing to offer anyone.

"I picked you because I could see inside your soul, and yes, you did have something to offer." "You are a unique person. Just like I am unique." I told her. Besides, everyone has something to offer."

"You are a special person, Lola, and don't ever forget about that. I hope our children have as much to offer someone special as well."

I looked at him and said, "Our children?" "You have never spoken about children before."

"You do not want children Lola?"

"Of course I do; I have not heard you speak That way until now."

"That is because I did not know where your head was then."

"I love you, Lola. Ben said."

"I love you too, Ben, I said."

We went to sleep in each other's arms.

In the morning, when we woke up, it was cold out, with a light coating of snow on the ground. We all took our time getting up. Ben started the fireplace, and we all sat around it. Shiloh asked when we were going to go looking for the portal again.

"We should go out tomorrow morning. We all need some time together. Don't you think? I know I want to spend the day with Ben. Don't you want to spend your time with Nick today?"

"Well, yes, Shiloh said. I want to find out where the portal is to get the information we need, too."

"I know, Me too," Lola said. "There is plenty of time to do that another time. Ben agreed with me, and we sat around the fireplace and chatted for a while."

"After everything ends with Morgan, I want to settle here and get a horse or two."

"Are you going to kill her, Lola?" Shiloh asked.

"I would rather not, but if I have to, I will. I said. I would rather be civilized about things, but if she gives me no choice, I have to do what I must to make everyone around me safe and myself."

"I hope you understand," Shiloh said.

"I do, but she is the only grandmother I know."

"I know," I said. I will talk to her first and try to work things out. I hope that works, but if it does not, we must be prepared to fight. Do you understand that, Shiloh? We will have to fight her."

"I do not like it, but I understand what and why we must do it," Shiloh said.

"For now, do not worry about anything, okay."

"Okay," Shiloh said.

"Let's go outside and spend some time on the porch now since it is a little warmer."

"Yes, let's take our drinks out with us and drink them out there." Let us not worry about anything right now. Let's have fun today. Tomorrow is another day, and we can worry about things then. Okay?"

"What can we do?" Shiloh asked.

"Ben, do you know of anything we could do?" Lola asked.

"Well, I do know of a lake we could go to. It is close to here. There is a hiking trail there, too."

"I like that idea," Shiloh said. "I like hiking."

"Well, hiking is it then," Ben said.

Everyone gets dressed warm enough to go hiking. Ben said. It is cooler over by the lake.

Okay, everybody said.

"I can't wait to go hiking," Shiloh said. "I have not been hiking since this whole thing started."

"I know, Lola said, and I am sorry for that."

"Do not be sorry, Lola," Shiloh said. "I would rather be safe than sorry."

We all piled into Ben's car and went to the lakeside trails. We walked all day long. We were tired when we got back home. It was late when we got home, so beforehand, we ordered some food so we did not have to cook. Then we watched a movie and drank some wine.

When the movie was done, we all went to bed. Shiloh and Nick went to their room, and Ben and I went to ours. When our door was shut, Ben said, "Get undressed, Lola; I want to worship your body tonight. I have missed you so much during the past week."

"I have missed you too. I said."

I know you said that you trusted me the last time we were alone together, and I hope that is still the case tonight.

"I want to tie you to bed and worship every part of your body." I saw the uncertainty in her eyes, but there was raw desire there, too.

"You know we do not have to do things my way if you do not want to."

"I know," she said. I have never been tied to a bed before."

"I know," he said. That is why I said we do not have to do it."

"I am finding my curiosity is strong, though. I want you to tie me up. I want to see what it feels like".

I whispered in her ear. "You kitten are going to be amazed at how you will feel. Especially with my mouth all over your body. When I am done with my mouth. Then I am going to fuck you into next Tuesday."

"I am growing impatient, so I undressed and got on that bed."

I did what he asked me to do. I got undressed and laid down on the bed. He did quick work and tied me to the bedposts with some of his ties.

"Are they too tight?" He asked.

"No, they are good," I said.

"Good," he said. He then started to tease my body with his tongue. He started at my neck, then moved to my breast and played with them for a while. I began to moan, and he went farther down, and the more he played, the more I squirmed and moaned.

"Kitten, are you enjoying yourself?"

"Yeeesss," she said as she moaned.

I looked at her with the wickedest smile and then started to tease her some more. I went lower still and reached the clit. If she were not tied to the bed, she would have landed on the floor. That was how much she was squirming now.

I want you to come into my mouth, and I want to taste you. That is all it took. She came hard, and I loved every bit of it. I let her come down off her orgasm high, and then I started again. She was so hungry for me that her body stirred again.

"I am not done with you just yet," I said. I told you; I am going to fuck you. I will take it easy when entering you for the first time, but I will not be able to hold off for long.

"You have tried my patience for far too long." I entered her, and I almost came on the spot. She was so tight that I had trouble holding on. I wanted her to come before me. This is all about her pleasure tonight. I pushed more profoundly, and she let out a scream.

"Are you all right?" I asked her.

"Yes, I will be okay. I knew that my first time would hurt some."

Should I keep going? I asked.

"Yes, the hurting will not last too long."

"God, Lola, you are so tight I don't know how long I will last." As I was saying it, she was at her breaking point, so I pushed on. When she orgasmed, she lit up in tinny little sparkles. It was like little diamonds were all over her body. I let her come down, and she started talking.

"My body is so tingley." She said. "I feel like I am floating in the air."

Chapter 13

I do not know how to describe it.

"Kitten, it is called an orgasm. Did you like what I was doing to you?"

"Yes."

Good, because next time, I am going to bend you over the bed and fuck you so hard you scream my name and call me God. I untied her and went to get a wet cloth and cleaned her up. I let the feeling come back into her limbs, and then we changed the bedding.

"Let us get some sleep," I said.

"Yes, I am so tired now." She said.

In the morning, when we woke up, I was so sore. I felt like a Mac truck hit me. "Holy shit, I am sore," I said.

"That is to be expected. I tied you up, and you were squirming all over the place. Well, as far as the ties would let you."

"I will have to have someone else go with Shiloh today. She wants to see if she can find the portal to the Fea world. We need to get moving on that."

"I know," I said. I will ask Nick to go with her. He will understand why when I let him know."

"Okay."

"Stay right there; I will bring breakfast to you."

"Okay," I said. It is not like I could move well anyway."

"Later, I will draw you a bath, and we can take a bath together."

I made breakfast, and we ate in the bedroom. After we ate, I drew a bath, and we took a bath together. I took the sponge and cleaned her up. After we were done, I dried myself off, wrapped a towel around me, and started to dry Lola off. I started at her shoulders and continued down the rest of her body. Stopping at every sensitive spot, I could think of and rubbing the soreness out of her muscles.

I asked Nick to go with Shiloh today. I told her. I figured that you wanted to rest for the day. They should be back soon.

"Okay, thank you for doing that," she said. I know that she wanted me to go with her. I feel so close to her. I do not understand why I have this feeling about her, though. I only know that she is connected to me somehow."

"Anything for you, Kitten, anyway; Nick was happy to go with her."

"They are getting close now. I said. I am happy for them. If it were not for Morgan, we could settle in and live in peace."

"Yeah, I know," Ben said. We will all get to do that as soon as everything is taken care of. Let us go and sit by the fireplace. I can make us some hot chocolate."

I sat by the fireplace while Ben made us some hot chocolate and just stared into the fire. It was mesmerizing. I was deep in thought when Ben sat down by me. As he sat down, he gave me my cup, and we drank silently. Shiloh and Nick came in and sat with us.

"Is there any more hot chocolate left?" Nick asked.

"Yes," Ben said. "Do you want me to get you and Shiloh some?"

"No, sir, I will get it," Nick said. I entered the kitchen, grabbed two mugs, and poured hot chocolate. I went back into the living room and handed Shiloh her cup and then sat down beside her, and we drank it by the fireplace.

After everyone was done drinking, the cups were empty. Lola cleaned up the dishes and came back to sit with us.

"Shiloh, did you find anything today?"

"No, but I do feel like I am getting close, though. The next time, I want you to come with me." She said. That means, Ben, no rough sex." I say with a smile.

"We can go out tomorrow," I told her. I want to find the portal as well. I need to know how we are related, and I need to know information on Morgan. "Shiloh, I don't remember if I told you she's my grandmother too.

"Yes, you did," Shiloh said.

"Well, she is. I said, and that was all my aunt got to tell me about her other than she is not so nice. So, now, why do I need this information? It is not a want anymore. It is a need. I need to know how you and I are related. It feels like my whole life has been one big lie."

"I know how you feel," Shiloh said. Me too. Maybe that's why Morgan killed your aunt. She probably thought that she was going to help you in some way or warn you."

"Maybe."

Okay, we will go tomorrow and search together. Shiloh said. I know that I am close. I can feel it. It may take one or two more days to find it, but we will find it. I am so determined to find this thing.

"So, Ben, how is everything going in LA?" Shiloh asked.

"If my staff would stop dyeing on me, everything would be great."

"I am so sorry that my grandmother is so evil." She said. "I was going down the same path until I saw the truth."

"It is not your fault, Shiloh, and do not let her get you down," Ben said.

"Let us watch a movie, we all said simultaneously."

"What should we watch?" Ben asked.

"No more spooky shit. I am over it now," Shiloh said. I do not like it anymore. Anyway, I have enough spooky shit in my life right now."

"I am in the mood for a romantic movie," Lola said. "Anyone else? It is better than nothing."

"Okay," we all agree and put on some love story.

After the movie was done, I headed to bed. Lola said. I want to be up early in the morning so I can go with Shiloh and see if we can find the portal that we need to find."

"Okay," Ben said. We all need some rest after the day we had. Ben was looking at Lola when he was saying it."

The movie was done, and everyone headed to their rooms.

I have the feeling that Morgan is on her way here again. I do not know when she is going to show up. I know everyone has been feeling the same thing.

This morning, when we woke up, we had a sense of forbidden. Something is off. "I do not know if we should look for this portal today," Lola said.

"I agree," Shiloh said, but if we do not do it now, we might not get another chance. It is not like these portals stay in one spot forever. They move around, and it is more difficult now because we are not on any of the equinoxes."

"Shit," Lola said. Do we have to go out today? I have this feeling that something is not right. I cannot put my finger on it, though."

"I know," Shiloh said. I feel it too, but we must do this."

By this time, Benn chimed in. "We will all go out. If we stay together and something goes wrong, we can fight it together."

"Agreed," everyone said.

We ate breakfast and got ready to go out. We packed some snacks and water and went into the forest.

"So, what are we looking for?" Ben asked.

"We are looking for anything that may look like a portal. It may be round or oval in nature. It will look like liquidity inside it. Like a liquid mirror and silver in color."

"Okay," Ben said. Am I the only one not knowing what we are looking for?"

"Yes," they all said at one time. Then started laughing. Let's get looking. I want to find this thing today. I still have the feeling that something is not right. I am starting to get a headache."

"Let's get going on with this already," Ben said. "I want to get this over with."

So, we all went into the forest and started looking for this portal that looked like a liquid mirror.

"I will be in the middle of a clearing," Shiloh said.

"Okay," everyone replied.

So, we set off looking for it. It was not too long, and we heard Ben shout.

"I think I found it." All of us look over his way. Then, I went over to him.

"How did you find it?" Shiloh asked.

"I nearly walked through it," Ben said.

"Shit," Shiloh said.

"I thought you said it would look like a liquid mirror," Ben said.

"I did," Shiloh said.

"Well, this one I couldn't see and almost walked through it. I didn't look like anything. It did not have a shape either. Just a tingling feeling when you come close to it."

"Wow, I did not expect that. Shiloh said. I have never seen that happen before. I know it is different for everyone, but that is unreal."

"Okay, now that we found it. What are we going to do?" Ben asked.

"I will see who is around and ask if Lola can come in with me." Unfortunately, only people that have the Fae blood can go in that world unless people are kidnapped and taken across into that world."

"Okay, we will wait here," Ben said. If something goes wrong, are you able to communicate with us?"

"Yes, but the only one that I would be able to communicate with is Lola because we both have the same gifts of sight clairvoyance."

"Okay," Ben said. Then do that, and I will send her in after you."

"Okay," Shiloh said, then went into the portal. "Lola, I am in their world now."

"She is in now," Lola said.

"I am talking to the head Farie here," Shiloh said

"Okay," Lola said. I am relaying everything you say to the guys."

"Lola, they said you can come in," Shiloh told her.

"Okay," Lola said. "Shiloh said they want to meet with me," I told Ben and Nick.

"Okay," Ben said. Remember, we cannot communicate with you when you are in that world. You will have to rely on yourselves and protect each other."

"Yeah, I know, I will be careful," She said.

"Hey, be careful when you step through that portal; it could be dangerous over there."

"Okay, I will remember that."

"Please do so; I don't want anything to happen to you. You are the only family that I have now.

I stepped through the portal, and it was like stepping through water. The portal was dense and felt like water. When I got to the other into the Fae world, it was nothing else I had ever seen. It was beautiful and lush with greenery. There were all types of fruit trees and flowers of all kinds.

There were fairies all over the place. In their world, they were the same height as humans, but they had wings.

They did not have to worry about people noticing their differences. In our world, they must disguise themselves. Someday, I want to go in and out of the two worlds. The Fairies exchanged satisfied glances before leading Shiloh and me deeper into the Fae world, where I could talk to the head Fae. The one that takes care of things when Morgan isn't around.

For now, I am happy to talk to them. I am now inside talking to the head fairy. I have so many questions. I told them I had no idea I was half Fae until I sprouted pointed ears one day and had a discussion with my aunt and had to drag the information out of her. Then I told them that Shiloh and I were related somehow but didn't know how. All we know is that Morgan is our grandmother.

I asked if they had any information on how we were related. They said that they would find out for us. I also told them Morgan was hunting me and the others with me. I asked them if they had any advice on how to defeat Morgan. I told them that I did not want to kill her. We need to make sure that she cannot harm anyone.

They told me that she only has the power of her staff, and if you somehow take the power of the staff or get it away from her.

She will not have the power to harm, but if you cannot get it away, you will have to fight her for it.

"Can I visit here when I want?" Lola asked.

"Wait until you defeat Morgan, and then you can visit anytime." They said. "We do not want to risk anything here. She is a powerful witch who would kill us if she knew we betrayed her."

"Okay, "I say. "Okay, Shiloh, I have to leave." "I look forward to any information you can give us about our relationship the next time we meet, which will not be for a while because we do not know when Morgan will show up at our doorstep."

"Okay, see you then," they said.

Shiloh and I left and went back through the portal, and then we were back in the mundane world. I looked at Shiloh, and we both said simultaneously, "Wow, that was intense." Then we gathered the guys up and went back to the house.

When we returned to the house, we told the guys what was said.

I told them that the fairies were willing to help Shiloh and I found out how we are related and that they gave us some advice on defeating Morgan. They said that her power comes from her staff, and if we could somehow take that power away from her, she would not harm anyone.

"Okay, at least we have something to go on," Ben said. "We need to start thinking up a plan to defeat Morgan now. She is coming, but I cannot tell when."

"I asked them if I could come into their world anytime, and they said I could, but I must wait until Morgan was defeated. They don't want to risk it. I must wait until everything is safe. So, that means that Shiloh and I have to wait to get the information on how we are related."

"Okay," Ben and Nick said. So, what should we do in the meantime?"

"Oh, I do not know, relax a little," Lola said. "I mean, we can start planning for Morgan's return, but I do not plan to get all out of sorts over her. Let us eat and get some rest tonight. We had an exceptionally long day."

"Okay, that sounds like a plan to me," Ben said.

We ate something and sat around the fireplace, chit-chatting for a while. Then Lola said that she was tired and that she was going to bed. Shiloh said the same.

"Okay, you girls go to bed," Nick and I will start planning something to defeat Morgan.

"Okay," they said. "Good night," they said and went to their rooms.

"Good night, Lola," Shiloh said before entering her room.

"Good night," Shiloh said.

I went into my room, and as soon as my head hit the pillow, I was out like a light. In the morning, when I woke up, Ben was still not in bed. I went out to see if he was still in the living room. I saw both sitting on the couch, sleeping with their heads bent backward on the back of the sofa.

It was all quiet in the house, and suddenly, I heard Shiloh scream.

The guys heard it, too, and jumped to a start. She came out of her room. "What the fuck is wrong with me?" I have wings. I was stretching, and they came out.

"Shiloh, calm down; it is just your Fae coming out," Lola told her. I know what it feels like. I freaked out when my ears came out.

Fortunately, that is all that came out of me. You have to be careful what you do. Your wings will come out when you least expect it. You must learn to control it."

"Holy shit," Ben and Nick say. I thought that I was going to have a heart attack. Do not do that to us again, please."

"You thought something was wrong with me," Shiloh asked.

"Yes," They all said. "You scared us half to death."

"Now that I know I am fine, I will not be scaring you anymore. I wish I knew that that was going to happen. I would have been better prepared for it. I hope that all that happens to come out.'

Time will tell, Lola said.

"Oh god," you mean to tell me that more features could emerge.

"Yes, that is what I am saying." "It still could happen to me too. Just know that I will be here for you. I will not let you go through this alone."

"Okay," I am glad I have you, Lola. "Without you, I would be lost."

"Oh, kiddo, I am so glad I met you, too. I love you."

"I love you too, Lola."

"Why don't we go hiking today?" Lola said. "I need some fresh air and to stretch my legs. I am quite sure that Shiloh would like to start practicing how to control her wings."

"Yes, indeed, I would like to practice."

"Lola, I do not think Shiloh should practice in the open," Ben said. "It is not safe."

"Oops, you're right. Shiloh, I will take you into the forest tomorrow to practice."

"Okay," she said.

We got dressed in warm clothes, piled into Ben's car, and went to the lakeside trails to go hiking. All the trees were the colors of fall. They were shades of yellow, orange, and brown. It was cool out but not so cold you could not stand it. When we got back home, all we wanted to do was sit by the fireplace.

"I will make some hot chocolate," Lola said. "Who wants a cup? Everyone told me all at one time. I made a big batch of it, and we drank until it was all gone. We stayed by the fire for a while longer, just absorbing all the heat."

"Well, I am headed to bed," Lola said. "I am wiped out. This was a good day. Good night, everyone."

"Me too," Shiloh said. "I will read before I go to bed, though. I also said good night to everyone and went to my room. I went to my room and popped open the book that I was reading a couple of days ago."

I must have fallen asleep with the book in my hands because when I woke up this morning, it was still there.

Everyone came out of their rooms, and we sat around, trying to wake up fully. "Good morning, everyone."

"Good morning to you, too," they all said.

"What are we doing today?" Shiloh asked.

"I am going to clean the house," Lola said. "It has been neglected for the last couple of days. Care to join me, Shiloh?"

"Sure, why not? I don't have anything else to do."

"Before we start cleaning, I am going to eat," Lola said. "I am famished. How about you? What do you want to eat? I am just having some toast and coffee."

"I will have the same," Shiloh said.

Ben and Nick both said that they were not hungry and that they would eat later.

Okay," I said and made Shiloh and me something to eat. We ate and then cleaned the house. When everything was done, I made some hot chocolate and Shiloh, and I sat by the fireplace. We drank in silence and then talked.

"I cannot wait to find out how we are related," Shiloh said.

"That makes two of us," Lola said.

"What are we planning for the return of Morgan?" Shiloh asked.

"Honestly, I do not know, "she said. "This whole thing with her has me all tangled up inside. I know that I should hate her with all my being, but at the same time, she is my grandmother."

"I know the feeling, and the struggle is real." "I mean, I want to hate her, but for whatever reason, I can't."

"I hope I do not have to fight her," Lola said. "If I have to, I will, though. I do not know the strength of my power yet. I am worried that if I must fight her, I might not have enough power."

"Do not worry, Lola, I will be with you all the way." "I will be by your side, and I will not let anything happen to you. I told her."

"Thank you, Shiloh," Lola said with tears.

Ben and Nick entered the room as we cried and hugged each other.

"What are you girls crying about?" They asked.

"We are just bonding," Lola said.

Ben turned to Nick and shrugged. "Woman, Nick said. I do not know if I will ever understand them."

"That makes two of us," Ben said.

"What were you two doing?" Shiloh asked

"Sparing," Ben said. "We must be able to defeat Morgan if the need arises."

"Speaking about training." "Shiloh, do you want to go out and try your wings out tomorrow?"

"Sure, why not," she said.

"Nick and I will be coming with you just in case something goes wrong."

Chapter 14

"Okay," Shiloh and I say.

"For now, we should relax and sit by the fire," Nick said.

"Sounds good to me," everyone said. "Tomorrow is a whole other day."

Sitting by the fireplace, we munched on something and talked about everything we did during the day. Then, the girls said that they were going to their rooms to read and get ready for bed.

"Nick and I are going to stay out here for a while," Ben said. We said good night and left to go to our rooms. I said good night to Shiloh, and she said good night back before she went into her room.

I, however, only got a little reading done. I could not concentrate on anything that I was reading. I put my book down and tried to get some sleep. That did not come easy, either. I was too worried about Morgan and what I might have to do.

Ben finally came into the bedroom, and he saw that I was still awake.

"Having trouble sleeping?" He asked.

"Yeah," I am worried about what we must do when Morgan finally comes for us. I am unsure of my powers, and I do not think Shiloh is ready to fight her grandmother."

"Yeah, I know; I am a little worried myself." "I did not want to say anything and upset everyone's day. "

"I wish you had said something; I would have voiced mine too." "Anyway, I must try to get some sleep. I promised Shiloh that I would help her train tomorrow."

"I know," Ben said. "It will suck to be doing it while you are tired. That's one of the reasons that Nick and I are going with you. I sensed that you were worried and that it might be the cause of no sleep. Let us try to get some sleep. Try not to worry so much."

"I will try; I have so much on my shoulders." "Ben, I must protect her because she is the only relative that I have."

"I know," Ben said. "We just have to make sure we take more precautions regarding her. Nick will help, also. I know he will do whatever it takes to ensure her safety."

"I know he will." "It is nice to see that you and your Nick are bonding. I was wishing that would happen.

"Get some sleep," Lola said.

When I finally got to sleep, I started to dream. I was in the middle of the forest, and suddenly, I was in a ring of fire. Then, this woman showed up and told me I would never be free of her. Then I feel this burning on my forearm in the shape of a feather. She was branding me. She finally removed the hood of her clock and showed me how she was.

"Morgan."

"Now, we are bound together forever."

I woke up screaming, and Ben woke up.

"What's wrong," Ben asked.

"I had a dream that Morgan branded me and bound me to her forever.

"Lola, It wasn't a dream."

I looked down at my arm, and sure as shit, the feather was there.

"What the fuck?" "Ben, look what she did to me; that, that bitch."

"Okay, calm down, Lola."

"Calm down, I can't calm down. Look what she did to me."

"I know, but we must explain to Nick and Shiloh, and you can't do it like this."

"Okay, you're right, but this scares me because I don't know what it means."

"We will ask Shiloh if she knows what it means," Ben says.

"What time is it," I ask him.

Unfortunately, it's time to get up; we must ask Shiloh what all this means."

"Unfortunately, I have to train with Shiloh while I am tired. I will not complain, though. I don't want to alert everybody to how much I am worried. I am glad that the guys are coming with us today."

"let's get.... I stop."

All of a sudden, there was a pounding on our bedroom door.

"Lola, what's going on? I had a dream last night that you and Morgan had it out.

"We will be out in a minute, Shiloh; I will explain when we come to the living room."

"By the way, Ben, thank you for coming with us today." That said, we went into the living room to talk to Nick and Shiloh. I explained to Shiloh that I encountered Morgan in my dreams or what I thought was a dream.

"Morgan has bound me to her."

"Holy shit, Lola, you will never be free of her now; this also means that you can't kill her either because to kill her, you will have to kill yourself. She made it so out of bounds. Did she brand you?"

"Yes, she left that mark of a feather on my forearm."

"That makes it worse; now she can sense where and what you are doing."

"Holy shit," at least I know where I am when it comes to her."

"No, you don't; just because she can sense you, it doesn't mean that you can always sense her; sometimes you might be able to, but it's not a guarantee."

"Okay, okay, I got it; let's go train; we have to get ready, Morgan, anyway." "I must put my psychic walls up to keep Morgan out of my head."

We ate something before going to train and packed some snacks and water. We went out to the forest, where we had room to move around. Shiloh started to train with her wings. At first, it was difficult for her, but she soon got the hang of it. She's a fast learner.

"How do you feel," Shiloh asked.

"More confident," she said. "I feel like I am doing better, and I am not going to freak out again."

"That is good," I said. "We still have a long way to go, though. I need you to get way better than you are right now. There is no room for mistakes. Do you understand?"

"Yes, I understand," Shiloh said. "Boy, you sure know how to rain on someone's parade," I said under my breath.

"I heard that."

"Okay," let's have another go at it, shall we." Suddenly, Shiloh shot up in the air like no other time that she was practicing and came back down on her feet.

"Good," I said. "That is going to be all that we do today. It is late, and I want to go back and relax for the rest of that night."

By the time we got back to the house, everyone was so tired that we just went to bed. We did not even want to eat. Ben and I went to bed, and when I finally got to sleep, I had another dream. This time, it was my aunt that was in my dream. She was calling me. In my dream, I found myself back out in the forest at the clearing.

"What are you doing here? You're supposed to be dead."

"I am, dear; I came here to warn you that you and your family are in grave danger." "Morgan will not stop until she kills you."

"I know, Auntie; I just don't know what to do about it." "She has bound me to her forever."

"You will have to find some way to defeat her without killing her because if you kill her, then you will kill yourself."

"I am well aware of that fact, Shiloh told me."

Then I woke up with a start. I only remember a little from the previous day. It was still too early to get up, so I went back to sleep. When I woke up for the day, I noticed my back was itching, and then, poof, I got my wings. I was so excited I wanted to tell Shiloh.

"Lola," Ben said. "I think that she will be sleeping."

"Oh, you are right." "It is just that I am excited to tell her that she is not alone with that wing thing anymore."

"I know," he said but waited until she woke up. You pushed her hard yesterday.

"I know, and now that I have wings, I will have her sparing with me." "After I know how to use them, of course. It will not take me long to get used to them."

"I know it will not," Ben said. "You are a quick learner."

I kept my wings out so I could get used to them, and when Shiloh came into the kitchen, she let out a squeal.

"You too," she said.

"Yes, me too," I said. "Now, you do not have to do it alone."

"Thank God for that," she said. "Now we can practice together."

"Yes, we can," I said. "The first thing you have to do is get used to them. Then we will start sparing to defeat whatever comes at us."

"I can't wait," Shiloh said. "Have you learned how to put them back in yet?"

Chapter 15

"No," I wanted to keep them out so you could see them. "I will learn that, though. I must because people in the mundane world are not used to seeing us. You must learn it, too."

"Already did; I am steps ahead of you." She said.

"Today, I want to rest," I told her. "We will go out tomorrow morning to practice."

"Okay," Shiloh said. "I want to read anyway."

"Ben and Nick are out in the woods sparing."

"Shiloh, do you want something to eat?" I asked.

"Some toast and tea will be fine, thank you."

I made us something to eat, and we sat by the fireplace and ate our breakfast. The guys came in shortly after we were done.

"Do you guys want something to eat?"

"Sure,' they said.

I made them something and then went into the kitchen to clean up. When I was done, I returned to the living room to tell them that Shiloh and I were going out to practice tomorrow morning.

"Okay, we will go with you." They said.

"Okay," I said and went about my business. "I am going to relax and read. Then I left to go to my room. Nick, Shiloh is in your room reading also. Thank God for books, or I would not know what to do with my time."

I finished the book that I started a couple of days ago and started a new one. I love to read. By the time I was done reading, it was time for dinner. I made something to eat, and everyone ate. Then we just sat by the fire, enjoying our time together.

"I am going to bed," Lola said. "I need to rest for tomorrow morning's practice."

I went into the bedroom, got ready for bed, and got under the covers. Then I popped open the book that I was reading earlier and started to read, but I must have fallen asleep. My book was still in my hand when I woke up this morning. I entered the living room, but I was still waiting for someone to be up.

I got dressed, went out into the living room, and quietly made something to eat. By the time I was done, Shiloh and Nick were leaving their room. We all sat at the table eating.

"Ben, did you come into the room last night?"

"Yes, but you were passed out on the bed, and I didn't want to bother you, so I came back out here and slept."

"Lola, are you ready to get going to practice?" Shiloh asked.

"Girl, I am so ready for this; my wings are itching and ready to come out."

"Let's do this," Shiloh said.

Everyone packed some snacks and water, and we went to the forest. We arrived at the perfect spot. We put our stuff down, and Shiloh and I started stretching our wings.

"What do you want to focus on today?" Shiloh asked.

"Well, since you already know how to put your wings back in. Can you teach me how to do that?"

"Sure," Shiloh said. "We have them out now, so just give the command in and think it in your head, and they should go back in."

"Okay," I said and did it. I told them to go in, and at first, they were hard to put in, and it felt weird to do, but the more I practiced, the easier it got.

"Okay," I got it now.

"Okay," Shiloh said. "Try it again without saying it aloud. Just think about it. I did as she told me, and they opened and closed with no problem. I did it."

"Is there anything else that you want to practice today?" Shiloh asked.

"No, we are good for today." "I am tired. Let's go home; we can come back out tomorrow."

"Sounds good to me," She said

"That was fun, and my wings didn't bother me when doing it."

Before we left, we sat and had a snack and water. By the time we got back to the house, we were tired. All I want to do is go to bed. The men stayed up, and Shiloh and I went to our rooms and went to sleep. I hit the pillow, and I was out like a light. I slept all night without getting up at all.

Chapter 16

This morning, when everyone woke up, it was a bright and shiny day. I went out onto the porch and took a big breath of fresh air in. Today is a brand-new day, I said to myself. Ben came out.

"I want to go hiking today. Are you up to it?"

"Sure," I am always up to a good hiking day. Let us see if Nick and Shiloh want to go."

"Sure, why not? The more the merrier."

Ben went back into the house, shouting for Nick and Shiloh.

"Do you want to go hiking today?"

"Sure," are we going to eat before we go?" Nick asked.

"Yes," I said.

We all ate and then packed snacks and water. We went on our way to the lakeside trials. On the way up the trail, I started to feel uneasy.

"Ben, I do not know what this feeling is, but I have been uneasy since we started hiking. It is a feeling I have never had before, and I cannot explain it."

"I had that feeling before. It is the feeling that something is going to go wrong. You do not know what, though. Ben said. I do not have it now, though. Are you feeling okay? Lola."

"I am feeling fine, and I do not feel ill." I just cannot put my finger on the feeling. It's my imagination. I have been worried about things going on here that I could be imagining the feeling."

"Maybe," He said.

"Oh well, let's continue our hike," shall we? "It will take my mind off it for now."

"Okay," Ben said.

We continued our hike and got to the top of the hill, and the view was so beautiful. We are looking down at the most beautiful forest that there ever was. The trees are all different shapes, sizes, and colors. We walked around for a while and then headed back down the trail, and I saw two black crows.

"I do not remember seeing them on the way up," Lola said.

"Me either," Ben said. "I wonder what they mean, even if they have a meaning."

"I will meditate on it when we get home," Lola said. "After we eat, though, I cannot do anything on an empty stomach."

We got home and ate some dinner, and I still had the feeling.

"Ben, I am going into our room to meditate in private. I went and set up for my meditation with the candles that I always use and started to meditate. At first, nothing came to me, but the more I strained to see into the future, it came.

"Lola, the crows are from me, your Grandmother Morgan." "They are my pets, and they are watching you for me. I will come for you soon, and I am not happy. I am going to kill you."

"I am sending a message to you, grandmother." "I know you can hear me. I won't stand for any violence from you on us. We did nothing wrong. If my crime is that I was born, that is not a good enough reason for you to come after me. I did not ask to be born into this."

"My dear Lola, I know you did not ask to be born into this, but I do not care." "I am coming after you anyway. Why, you ask? My answer is simple: because I can, and I will."

"Grandmother, I am closing this session and left the conversation."

I blew out my candles and went to tell the others what had transpired in my meditation.

"We better get ready for Morgan to come. She is coming, and she is coming with a vengeance. I told her that I did not ask to be born into this, and she flat told me that she did not care and was coming after me anyway. She knows every move that we are making. Those crows are hers, and they have been spying on us."

"Shiloh, tomorrow we are going to train."

"Okay," she said.

"We are also going to train tomorrow, Nick," Ben said.

"Okay," he said.

"For now, let's get some sleep," Ben said. We all agreed and went to bed. Everyone was tired from the hike anyway. Everyone went to their rooms. When Lola and I entered our room, I asked her if she was okay.

"I am fine," she said. "Morgan is after me but will kill anyone that gets in her way of killing me."

"I know," Ben said.

"I am worried about Shiloh. She doesn't have any fight time, nor have I, but I am wiser. Plus, Morgan has manipulated Shiloh in the past."

"I know, but try and remember that when Shiloh became aware of what was going on, she made the right choice and came to our side."

"I know," but we do not have that much training time. I do not know when Morgan is coming. She just said that she was coming soon. We need to be prepared to fight her. She won't stop until she is defeated somehow. At this point, I don't know if we can beat her."

"Don't think like that; you know that we must defeat her. I don't think that Morgan will stop at just us. The whole of humanity is at stake here."

"I knew that was a possibility too. I do not know what to do about it.

"You are not alone in this. We are all in this together. I am with you. We will all fight together. Let's get some sleep tomorrow on a new day."

"I am so tired," she said. "I need the deepest and nicest sleep that I can get." That is all I heard from her because she hit the pillow and was out like a light. As I lay beside her on the bed, wondering, "How in the hell are we going to defeat Morgan." I must have drifted off to sleep because the last thing I remember was the thought of Morgan. When we woke up this morning, everyone was in the weirdest mood. We all knew what was coming.

"We must train as much as we can before Morgan comes."

"It's so cold out today, and It feels like hell is going to freeze over."

"Well, before I let that happen, I will kill Morgan."

"Shiloh, it is time to train, and it's time to get serious on the training thing. We all do."

"We know," we all say at the same time.

"Okay, so let us do this," Ben said.

"Hell, yeah, let's do this," Shiloh yelled.

We went into the forest at the clearing and started training.

"Okay, who is first?" Lola asked. "Who wants to come to me? She asked again. Oh, come on, we must get going on this. We do not have time for you to lolly gagging around."

"Okay, you do not have to get testy about it, Lola."

"Well, how do you want me to act?" "No one is moving, and we must be prepared."

"I know we do," Ben said. "Okay," let us do this; I will be the first."

"Okay, come at me from the front first. Then you can come to me from the back."

"All right."

He came running, and I stood my ground and flipped him over my shoulder.

"Where did you learn how to do that?" Ben asked, confused.

"I watched a lot of T.V. shows with some moves like that. I am an adaptive learner."

"I guess so."

"Okay, come at me from the back."

He ran towards me, and I quickly spun around and kicked him. He went flying into the air.

"Holly shit, women, you are going to kill me."

Chapter 17

"Anyone else wants to try?" Lola asked.

"Hell No!"

"Shiloh, you and I have to spar."

"I do not know how to do that kind of stuff."

"Well, you are going to have to learn." "So, let's hit it. I will go easy on you because you don't know a lot. After you learn, though, it is no hold, bard, okay. I am going to come running towards you and you. Stop me at any cost."

"Okay."

"I hope that you are ready. Here I come."

I ran toward her, and she blocked me and threw me over her shoulder.

"I thought you said that you did not know any of the stuff that I just did?"

"I also learn quickly," Shiloh said. "I did not know I had it to do that."

"Okay," let's try the other move.

As I ran towards her, she braced for impact again; then she tried the other move that I did. She nailed it on the spot.

"Okay," now that part is over, Shiloh. "You and I have to do this while we are flying."

"All right," she said.

So, we sprout our wings and get up in the air. As we got up in the air, she asked me if Grandmother Morgan was watching us.

"I do not see her crows, but that does not mean anything. They could be off in the distance. Just keep a watchful eye."

"God," it feels great to release my wings and fly," Shiloh said.

"It feels great for me too."

"Well, if they are watching, she will know our moves."

"Yes, that is why we will use different moves." The moves that we are doing now are just for practice."

Okay, so we did the same moves on the ground. Everything was good, and we knew how to fight as best as possible. I was satisfied that we could beat her if the need arose.

"Come on, let's go home," Lola said. I am tired. When we got home, I was so tired that I was beyond exhausted. I was wiped out. Even though I had fun today, and it felt good to stretch out my wings, I have no energy left in me today.

"Did I say that I was tired?" Lola asked.

"Yes," Ben said.

"Well, fuck that shit. Lola said. I am fucking wiped out."

"Me too, Shiloh said. I want to go to bed."

"You do not want anything to eat, Shiloh? Nick asked.

"No, I just want my bed."

"Me too, "Lola said. You and Nick are all on your own tonight. Have fun cooking," I said.

Then, I went to my room to go to sleep. I must have gone to sleep right away. I do not remember anything after I went to my room.

When I woke up this morning, Ben was lying beside me. "When did you come to bed?" "I did not even feel or hear you enter the room."

"I know you didn't. I did not want to wake you, so I came in quietly. You passed out. I doubt that you would have felt or heard me anyway."

"Well, good morning. I said. I am starving."

"Well, it is no surprise you have not eaten since yesterday morning." Let's make some breakfast.

Nick and Shiloh were already out there when we went to the living room. "I am so hungry, Shiloh said.

"I am going to make some breakfast," Lola said. I am starving. I am going to relax today. I do not think anything is going to happen today. My body is protesting every move that I make."

I can feel every muscle in my body, even muscles I did not know I had.

Shit, me too, Shiloh said. My body has been protesting ever since you started training me, Lola. Shiloh said. I want to sit around and be lazy today. This is going to be my lazy day for the week.

Yes, let us sit around and relax today and be lazy, Ben and Nick said.

Let us eat by the fireplace. Ben said. Then I am going to go out and do some yard work. I hope you do not think I can be lazy. I am used to working, so I have to do something, or I get bored quickly. We ate, and then Ben and Nick went to do yard work. Shiloh and I sat on the porch and watched the men work.

I do not know about you, but I could not help even if I wanted to. I am just too damn sore. Lola said to Shiloh.

That is precisely how I feel, Lola. I hope this soreness does not last too long. We have yet to determine when Morgan is going to show up. Oh, that reminds me. Could you block Morgan from hearing your thoughts, Lola?

No, you didn't, Shiloh, but I can, and I do all the time because I don't need her in my thoughts or reading them. I learned how to do it a while back. I thought I told you. Do you know how to do it? I asked her.

Yes, I had to block her because she was meddling too much in my life. Shiloh said I cannot wait for this thing with Morgan to end. I want to get back to living my life.

Tell me about it; I want to get to mine, too.

What are we going to do when Morgan comes for us?

I still do not know, but I do know that we must fight her. That much of which, I am sure. I wish we did not have to be tough. I see no way around it. Her being the way she is. I am sorry, Shiloh, I have no choice but to fight her.

I know I wish that she would listen.

Me too,

Me too, the guys, "then we would have to go through all this shit. I am so sick of her already."

Lola, can you make us some hot chocolate, please? Ben asked.

Sure, I can. Who else wants some? She asked. Everyone said yes. I will make enough for seconds. Okay, everyone said. We love the way you make it anyway.

I will let you know when it is done. Then we can sit around the fire pit and drink it. I love being outside. Then I am going to clean up and go to bed. I have not been sleeping well in the last week. I have been worried about Grandmother Morgan and when she plans to come for us.

Shiloh and I can block her from our thoughts, but I am unsure about you or Nick. If she can read your thoughts, she will know all our moves and what we are doing.

Oh, my God, Lola. Why didn't you tell us earlier? We could have practiced our skills on that. We have that skill, but we must hurry to hone it in. Hey Nick, I hope you still know how to block people from your thoughts. We are going to need it soon.

Shit, man, I have not used that in a long time. I haven't had to. Well, you better practice getting better at it. We are going to need it. I have to do the same because I have not used mine either. I wish you had talked about this earlier. It would have given me more time.

Sorry, man, I just found out myself. Lola just told me. We can start practicing tomorrow. I am too tired to do it now. I am going to go to bed early tonight. I have been so nervous for the last couple of weeks. I could not do it anyway.

We drank our hot chocolate, talked by the fire pit, and tried to relax.

That is it, Lola said. I am tired of this Bitch recking everything. I am going to block her from my mind. She can go straight to fucking hell for all I care. Fuck her and the broom she rides in on.

Everyone stared at me. What? I said. I am so over her and the shit she is playing. We cannot have everyday lives because of the shit she is pulling. If she is going to do something, she should do it and get it over with.

Testy are we, Ben said.

Well, what do you expect? I am tired, and I have not slept well for weeks now.

I know, none of us have, Ben said. I am just surprised that sort of thing came out of your mouth. You are usually the calm one, or at least it seems like it.

Yes, well, everyone has their breaking point. I have just come to mine. She has pushed me to the bring. When she does come, I must tame my anger so I do not do anything stupid. I do not want anyone to get hurt because of me.

No one is going to get hurt because of you. Ben said. Let's get some sleep. Tomorrow is another day. Let's not worry about shit that we cannot control.

That is easier said than done. Lola said.

I know that, but we can try. Ben said.

Then we went to bed. When we got up this morning, I felt better than I did the previous day.

Shiloh, how do you feel?

I feel much better today.

Do you want to stretch your wings and fly for a while tomorrow?

Sure, she said.

Okay, after we eat in the morning, we will go out. Today, I don't want to do anything except cook food so we can eat. Shiloh and I spent the day doing whatever we wanted. Nick and Ben did whatever they wanted. When we were all done, it was time to go to bed again. We ate a little something; then we were off to our rooms to go to sleep. Unfortunately, I never get to sleep until early in the morning. I always try to get to sleep, though. By the time I went to sleep, it was time to get up.

I got up and ate with everyone else. I did not want to go out today, but I told Shiloh that we would go out today. I am so tired that I lack energy, but I will do my best when we are out.

Shiloh, are you ready to go? I asked.

Are you sure you want to go out? Lola. You look so tired, and I do not want you to hurt yourself.

I will be fine once we are up in the air and flying. Lola said.

We went into the forest where the clearing was and stretched our wings.

Let us do this, Lola said. I am already feeling better.

Shiloh shot up into the air first, and I followed. God, it feels so good to fly just for fun. It takes all my worries away for the time. I love the feeling that flying gives me. It's so freeing.

"I love it too, Shiloh said. I love the air going through my wings and the smell of the air, too.

Are you two ever going to come back down? Ben asked.

Yes, why, Lola said. What time is it?

You have been flying for about two hours now.

Wow, how time flies. Lola said. Get it, flies by?

Ha-ha, so funny. Ben said.

Okay, let's go home. Lola said. I am hungry anyway.

We went home, and by the time we ate and sat by the fireplace for a while, it was time to sleep. We all went into our rooms. For me, it was the first time in a long time that I got some sleep. As soon as I hit the pillow, I must have gone to sleep because I do not even remember going to sleep.

When I woke up this morning, I felt refreshed and ready for the day ahead. I did the chores for the day, and then I went flying by myself. It felt so good to be by myself that I took my time going back to the house.

Where were you? Ben asked.

I went out flying. Lola said.

Please do not go out by yourself next time. Ben said. It is not safe.

I will go with you.

Okay, I said. It just felt so good to go by myself, and I did not want to bother anyone to go with me.

I know, Lola, but you can always come to me. Ben said.

Okay, Lola said. I will get you the next time I want to go out alone. I cannot wait to go out without feeling like I am a nuisance to everyone.

You are never a nuisance to me, Lola. Ben said.

I know, but I feel like I am.

I will try and connect with Morgan to see what is going on. I don't think that she is going to let on about she is coming, but it's worth a try. I feel so good, and I think the connection will be a good one for me. I told everyone I was going to my room to connect with Morgan and needed privacy. They all agreed not to disturb me.

I will let you know what is going on when I come back out. I go to the bedroom, light my candles, and put them in a circle around me. I then called out to Morgan.

Morgan, I want to talk to you.

What do you want? Lola.

Why are you toying with us? We know that you are coming for us. Why drag it on?

I am doing it because I can. You will not have that much longer, though. I am becoming bored, and I am coming to kill you in a couple of days.

That is all I want to know. Lola said. I am closing this circle now. Good by Morgan. I close the circle and blow out the candles. Then, I went to tell everyone what was said.

Okay, I got the information. Lola said. Morgan is coming for us in a couple of days. She said that she is becoming bored with toying with us. She is planning to kill me. What she doesn't know is that we are prepared for her to come after us.

I have kept her from going into my mind and reading my thoughts. I also know that Shiloh has blocked her also. Even if Morgan did know what we had planned for her, we could use a different strategy.

Shiloh, tomorrow will be our last day to train. Are you up for it? Lola asked.

Sure, Shiloh said.

We have to make this training a good one. It is the last one before Morgan comes for us.

Yeah, I know. She said. I am ready to take on any training you have for me to do. I realize that this training is going to be intense also.

Yes, it will. I said. We are likely to be sore for a couple of days. Even when we have to fight Morgan, it is all worth it, though. When we defeat her, we will be free of her if we do not kill her. We have to make it at least so she cannot harm anyone.

Remember, you can't kill her because you will be killing yourself in the process.

It will feel good to be free of her, Shiloh said.

Yes, it will, everyone else said.

Let us make the best out of today, though. Lola said. I am going to make today a lazy day. I do not want to do anything. Right now, I want to go outside and sit by the fire pit with some hot chocolate. It has been chilly lately, and I enjoy the cooler weather. I don't give a rat's ass what Morgan is right now. I want to relax today.

I made enough hot chocolate so we could have seconds if we wanted it. Then we went out by the fire pit and sat. We contemplated the days to come.

I want to make everyone here know that when Morgan comes, someone will get hurt or, even worse, killed. This is serious shit which we are dealing with. Morgan will not stop until I use my power to heal someone. That is what she wants because then she has just cause to try and kill me.

Even if she tries to kill me, I have one thing that will help me defeat her. I can block her from my mind so she will not know the next move.

That I am going to make, and so do all of you.

The only other time that Morgan can connect with me is when I am sleeping. That is when my wall is down. She has tried to communicate with me, though, for which I am glad. I would be stressed out then.

I want to finish this and go back to living my life. Lola said.

We all want our lives back, Shiloh said. I cry every night because I feel horrid. After all, she had me believing that you were the bad guy.

Oh, Shiloh, come here I said. Then I gave her a great big hug. You are not to blame for this. Girl, you are making me cry now.

Please do not cry, Shiloh said. You are going to make me cry again.

Well, I will lock myself in the bedroom for the rest of today, Lola said. Are you cooking for the rest of the day? I want to relax and read a book, which I have not done.

Yes, we are good. Shiloh said. God, and do what you want to do.

Oh, I plan on it. I said.

I went into my and sat in my favorite chair. I took the book I started reading a couple of weeks ago, popped it open, and started reading. I read it until I finished it. Then I went out to see if Ben was going to come to bed and went back to my room. Ben came in shortly after and kissed me hard.

What was that for? I said breathlessly.

Oh, because you are you. He said. I love you, Lola.

I love you too, Ben. What am I in the mood for?

No, what? Ben asked.

I am in the mood for you to give me a good fuck tonight. I said.

I leaned into her ear and said, "Are you now? Ben said. Well, then, you better get that pretty ass undressed.

I told you last week that I was going to bend you over the bed, and that is precisely what I plan to do tonight.

I got undressed slowly and made every move as sensual as I could. I took off my shirt first and dropped it to the floor. Then, my pants were the second thing to go. I slowly took off my bra and dropped it to the floor. He came to me.

Let me take the rest of it. He said. I took her panties off, and then I kissed her. I told her to turn around and face the bed. I tied her to one of the bed posts with one of my ties and bent her over. Not entirely over the bed but slightly over it. Half of her body was over the bed, and the bottom half was in the air. I slapped her ass. "You know that you are a dirty little girl."

Do you want more? I asked.

Yes, she said.

I gave her another couple of smacks, and she was panting hard.

Do you want me to fuck you?

Yes, she said.

Get ready, Lola, I am going to fuck you so hard that you will be screaming my name. I entered her from the back. God, Lola, you are so damn tight. You feel so good around me. I love the way you fit around my cock. I am going to fuck you into next week. As she moaned, I began to push faster.

Harder, she said. I almost lost it then and there. I gave her what she wanted. I pushed harder and deeper. She screamed my name as she was coming. I came after her.

That was intense, she said.

Yes, it was, He said.

I love fucking you, Lola. I untied her and rubbed the feeling back into her wrists, and we laid down on the bed. Let's get some sleep. We have training tomorrow morning.

Yes, let's do that. We went to bed, and I slept all night long. When I woke up in the morning, I felt refreshed and ready for training.

Good morning, Ben.

Good morning to you, too. He said. Are you ready for today? He asked.

Yes, I am so ready for training today.

Let's see if everyone else is up so we can eat. He said. We went out into the living room, and Shiloh and Nick were already out there. We made something to eat and sat at the fireplace to eat it.

Hey, are you ready to train today? Lola said.

Yes, bring it on, everyone said.

Okay, we packed some snacks and water, and we were off deep into the forest where the clearing was. Let us do this.

Who is coming for me first? Lola asked.

I will, Ben said. I ran towards her, and she spun and kicked me, and I dropped down so fast. Damn, she is fast, I thought to myself. I hope she is fast enough to beat Morgan.

Chapter 18

Again, she said. I ran towards her again, and she flipped me over her shoulder. This time, it took me a while to get up. I hit the ground with a thud, knocking the wind out. I looked over and saw that Nick and Shiloh were practicing their moves, too.

Okay, everyone, it is time for Shiloh and me to practice our flying.

Shiloh, are you ready to fly?

Yes, I am.

Okay, girl, show me what you got. I say to her. She came running towards me, and I thought she would run right into me, but her wings came out, and she flew straight up into the air—oaky, Great, Shiloh. I said. You can come back down. You are good at flying. I have just one question, though. Why do you have to get a running start?

I don't; I like the dramatic feel of it.

Oh, you, come here so I can give you a nuggy.

She smiled, I love you, Lola.

Love you too, Shiloh. I gave her that nuggy that I told her I would give her.

Okay, we are as ready as can be to fight Morgan if we have to. Lola said. Let's go home and make the most of the day.

Okay,

"That bitch has stolen all of our lives. Especially mine since she has bound me to her. I don't sleep well because she is always there in my mind.

By the time we got home, it was time to eat. I made something, and we sat around the fire pit outside and ate. When we were done, I cleaned up. We were all inside now.

Does anyone want hot chocolate?

Yes,

We drank it, and then everyone went to their rooms for the night.

Let's get some sleep, "I have no idea when Morgan is coming. I cannot wait until we can live everyday lives.

Me too,

We went to bed, and I tried to sleep but couldn't because I was worried about tomorrow. I hope everything goes as planned and no one gets hurt. When I got to sleep, it was time to get up. I only had an hour's sleep. Even though I got only that hour, I was surprisingly awake. It is the adrenaline pumping through my veins.

I know Morgan is coming for us today, but I do not know when, and it bothers me. I have even tried to reach out to her, but this time, she has blocked me out. I am keeping my mind open so I can hear her coming.

Ben, I feel sick.

It is your nerves.

No, this is something else. I told him. I am so sick I feel like I am going to throw up. That is something that I have never felt before. After I eat, I feel like this too. I have been feeling like this for about three weeks now.

It worries me because we only have one chance to do this right.

I know, he said. Do not worry so much. We will get this right the first time because we have no choice.

I am so whacked out of my head right now. She said. I know that we will defeat her, but I still have my doubts that we will do it without someone getting hurt or, worse, killed.

"I know there will be injuries, but I also hope that there are not any deaths. I do not want anyone to die. Ben said.

"How are you feeling," Lola said.

"I still feel sick, I say.

"I wonder what it could be?" You said the feeling has been with you for about three weeks now. I wonder if you could be pregnant."

"Oh my god, I have not thought about that," I do not have the time to think about it now either. I will think about it after everything is taken care of."

You know, if you are, you should not fight.

"I know, Shiloh, but I don't have a choice now. I will be careful what I do. If she started hurting people, I would put a stop to it right away somehow. I'm curious why I have been so hungry lately.

"That could be the reason," Ben said.

"Lola, who is Summer?" Shiloh asked. "I keep getting the name in my head, and I know I do not know anyone by that name."

"I do not know. Have you heard the name before and just remembering now?"

"No, I have not heard the name before." "Well, we will find out if I keep hearing it."

I guess, I say." "I am hungry, and I want to do something, but I do not know what I want."

"Well, that is the first," Ben said. "You always know what you want to eat. There is something going on with you, then."

"What do you mean, Ben?" Shiloh asked.

Well, I think Lola might be pregnant. Ben said.

"That explains the name then," Shiloh said. "The baby told me her name."

"Are you sure?" Lola asked.

"This is the first time I heard it, so yes, I am sure," Shiloh said. "What are you going to do with Morgan now that you know that you are pregnant?"

I am still going through with the fight if I have to if that's what you are asking. "I will be careful of what I am doing." "I have to now; my child's future is at stake."

"That is why your emotions have been out of order," Shiloh said. "You know that Morgan will know that you are pregnant." "She will be able to sense that baby."

"Yes, I know; I must tread carefully when dealing with her." "I want pickles."

"Okay, now, I know you're pregnant." "My mother craved pickles when she was pregnant with Nick."

"Do you have pickles on your planet?" Lola asked.

We had something like them, yes. Ben said.

Nick, take my car and get some pickles. Hurry, though; we have yet to determine when Morgan is coming.

"Okay, I will be right back."

"I hope Morgan comes soon," Lola said.

"Why," Ben asked.

"Because I am in the mood to kick some ass."

Nick got home just in time. He just pulled into the driveway when I came out of the house.

"Nick, Lola said that Morgan is on her way here,"

Okay, let us do this. Nick said. "We must protect Lola at all costs."

We are all outside now, waiting for Morgan to show up. Everyone was tense, and emotions were high. Waiting for Morgan is like going to the doctor. And I hate doctors.

"She is here," Lola said. "She is not happy that I am pregnant." "That means that she has another reason to kill me." "She is angry at me. She also knows that you are from a different planet, Ben."

"What does my being from a different planet have to do with it?"

"It has everything to do with it." "Our child will be a hybrid and stronger than normal Fae, which is not good for her." "That means if someone is more powerful than she is, she won't be fine with it." "Let us get into fight mode."

"Ah, I see you are ready for me," Morgan said.

"Yes, we are."

"You know, I know that you are pregnant." Don't you, Lola? Morgan said.

"Yes, I know that you know."

"So, you are still going to fight me?" Morgan asked.

"You're damn right I am. I have a child to protect now."

"Enough with the small talk," Lola said. "Let us get this over with, shall we?"

"Fine, Morgan said; you know what I want from you." "I want to come over to my side, The side of darkness."

"Yes, I know, but what you want and what you get are two different things." "I will never join forces with you."

"Then you will die," Morgan said.

"You can try killing me, but you will not succeed."

"Then let us get on with it," Morgan said.

She pulled out her staff, and it blazed bright with a magical current that became an electrical charge that shot out at us.

"While we are fighting, Morgan, keep all your thoughts guarded," Lola said. We blocked her first move.

"We have to try and tire her out," Lola shouted. "Then we can start making our move on her."

Morgan made another move, this time at Shiloh. She tried to knock Shiloh off balance and put her to the ground. It did not work, though. Shiloh was ready for the move.

Morgan went after Ben next because she knew that he did not know anything about her fighting tactic. She was successful at knocking him to the ground, and she focused on him. She knows that he is all in my life, and she will not let go. While still focused on Ben, she stretched out her other hand, shot a lightning bolt, and took out Nick. Shiloh tried to get to him, but Morgan blocked her.

Morgan froze Shiloh in place and then refocused back on the task at hand. Nick started to get back up, but Morgan quickly knocked him back down. This time, he stayed down. He was out cold. She was still very much focused on Ben at the time. He tried to get up But, Morgan would not let him. She walked over to Ben and kicked him in the stomach, and Ben went into a fetal position from the pain.

Nick started to get up again, and Morgan quickly knocked him down again, and this time, she made sure he stayed down. She walked over to him and kicked him in the stomach. And the sheer force of the kick broke his ribs. She went back to dealing with Ben.

"Lola, are you sure you do not want to come to the dark side and be by my side?" "We could conquer the world. Oh, what a time that would be. You and I are making people bend to our will."

"I will never come to your side."

"Oh, well, I guess Ben will have to die then." Then Morgan started to bring up that electrical ball of light in her staff. Still, before she could discharge it, Lola screamed, "Enough," and then her whole body started to vibrate and shine. Then she let out a big burst of energy, and the fight was over, and Morgan was knocked on her ass and out cold.

I took her staff and had it in my hand and when she woke up from being knocked out cold. She looked at me in confusion and asked, "Why and how did you get my staff."

"I took it when I knocked you out and on your ass. I will put it in a safe place so you cannot find it again. You can go back to whatever hole that you came from." Lola said.

Morgan hunched her shoulders and backed away slowly. But before she left, she said, "I will be back when you least expect it." She retreated into the forest and went back through the portal.

"Is everyone okay?" Lola asked. I was looking around at the group. Ben was still curled up in a ball, holding his stomach. Nick was slowly getting back up, wincing in pain. Shiloh was still frozen in place, but she was now starting to thaw out. I walked over to Shiloh and helped her out.

"Are you okay, Shiloh?"

"Yes, thank you."

"Are you okay, Lola?" I said as I looked at her stomach.

"I'm fine," I say as I smile at her.

I went to Ben and, using my healing energy, healed him. I bent over him and concentrated on my point, made a big ball of energy, and sent it into Ben's body. He slowly came to and started breathing.

"I'm sorry, Ben, I didn't know she would go after you like that." Feeling guilty for not being able to protect him. Then I started crying.

"What are you crying about," Woman? Be asked.

"I thought I lost you."

"I am here, a little sore, but I am here."

"Shiloh, How's Nick?" Lola asked.

"I think that he has some broken ribs, and I think he will be okay."

"Okay, let us get the guys inside to rest."

"Okay," Shiloh said.

We took the guys inside and then made them sit on the couch before the fireplace. I built the fire up so they could feel the warmth go through their bodies.

"Shiloh, I am going to make some soup so we can eat."

"Okay, but before you leave, tell me one thing. How in the hell did you defeat Morgan all by yourself?"

"I do not know," she said. It was like I had no control over what I was doing. I felt as if my body was acting all on its own. All I know is that I do not...."

"Be quiet for a minute, Lola," Shiloh said. "So, I can hear Summer. She is talking to me. Summer just told me that she helped you."

"Holy shit," Lola said. That means that she is going to be a powerful being."

"Yes."

"Well, let me get going with the soup. Lola said. I am hungry. Our men should be hungry also, as we have been through today. I want to eat and go to bed. Tomorrow is another day."

"Yes, I agree," Shiloh said as we entered the kitchen.

"Why did Morgan say she will be back?" Shiloh asked.

"Because I am going to have a powerful baby, and she wants to kill her. I replied.

"Do you think she will come back?"

"Yes, I do; she always has the power to return."

"Let us make sure that she does not hurt Summer."

"I will never let Morgan hurt Summer," So put your mind at ease. I was still in the kitchen, and Shiloh went back into the living room and sat with Ben and Nick and sat with them. We have the next few days to heal and get our energy back.

"It's going to feel nice to get back to our lives before Morgan became such a pain in the ass," Shiloh said.

Agreed, everyone said.

We ate by the fireplace tonight because everyone was pretty banged up from the fight with Morgan, and we did not have it in us to move around. When we were done, we stayed by the fireplace and just enjoyed the fire for a while more. Then, it was time to go to bed.

"Jeez, I feel like I got hit by a Mac truck. Lola said. How is everyone feeling?" She asked.

"About the same as you feel," they all said.

"Let us get some sleep," Lola said.

Everyone went to their rooms for the night. "I am so tired that I think I could sleep for two days straight," I tell Ben.

"We all are in the same boat,"

I laid my head down on the pillow, and that was it. I must have fallen asleep right away. When I woke up, Ben was still sleeping. I let him sleep, and I went out to make something to eat. Everyone started waking up one by one. First, Shiloh, then Ben and Nick were the last ones out.

"How is everyone feeling this morning?" I asked.

"Better than yesterday."

"I think for the next few days, we will stay home and do nothing," Lola said.

"I cannot agree more," Ben said. Doing nothing so good after what we have been through for the last few weeks."

"Morgan will be back; she has said so. She is not done with us yet."

"What does she want now?" Ben asked.

"She wants Summer."

"Over my dead body."

"She wants her because she will be a powerful being."

"What do you mean, a powerful being?"

"I thought I told you our child will be extremely powerful because she is a hybrid being. She has your blood and my blood in her. You are from a different planet than me because I am of Fea. Morgan will come and try to collect her like she did me. Or she will try and kill her."

"When that time arises, then we will take care of it. There is no use in worrying about it. "

"These few days flew by quickly, didn't they?" Lola said. Shiloh, do you want to see if the Fae we discussed a couple of weeks ago have any information on how we are related?"

Yeah, I do; I am curious now."

We went deep into the forest where the portal was. We called upon Fae to come to us this time. They went through the portal and asked what we needed.

"Did you find out how Shiloh and I are related?"

"Yes, we have." "We have found that you two are sisters."

"What, how?" we asked.

Your mother was dating a Fae before she met your father," "Lola. Your father fell in love with your mother and married her anyway. As for you, Shiloh, you have the same mother but not the same father. Your mother was separated from your father and went back to the Fae man that she was dating and got pregnant again." "You see, your mundane father took both of you in because he loved your mother with all his heart. Unfortunately, for some reason, they couldn't keep you, Shiloh, and gave you up. We will keep our ears to the ground to see if we can find anything else and then let you know."

"We said thank you," and then they went back through the portal and disappeared.

"Wow, I did not see that coming." "I thought they were going to tell us that we were cousins or something like that."

"Me too." "Well, that was a surprise.

"Yes, it was," I replied. "Let's go back to the house. When we got back to the house, our men were waiting on the couch by the fireplace for us."

"Well,' what did you find out?" Ben asked.

"We are sisters, same mother but different fathers from before and after they were married. My father is from the mundane world. Shiloh's father is from their world."

"Wow, I did not see that coming."

"We did not either. "At least you know now how you are related.

"Yes," Shiloh replied. "And I am so happy that I have a sister. It also explains why I was drawn to her." "Now we can move on with our lives and prepare for the baby to come."

"Yes, I cannot wait until she is here," Lola replied.

"She," Ben asked with a raised eyebrow.

"Oh, yeah, I did not get to tell you with everything else going on. Shiloh heard the baby speak to her. The baby's name is Summer. She is the one who stopped Morgan. She is powerful, even at this stage."

"Well, I will have to thank her when she is here for saving my life."

"Just talk to her now; she can hear you," I replied. "Come over here, touch my stomach, and talk. She will know that it is you somehow."

I went over and touched Lola's stomach like she said. "Thank you, little one, for saving my life, and she moved."

I told you that she would know you." "She knew me, and I did not even know it. I am so glad that we can live our lives now. Well, at least until Morgan decides to come back. That will not be for a while. In the meantime, I will live life to its fullest."

"Shiloh, do you want to go stretch your wings tomorrow?" I asked.

"Sure, why not."

"Do you think that is a good idea, Lola? Ben asked.

"I am pregnant, not injured," I replied. Knowing where this conversation was going.

Chapter 19

"That's my point. Should you be flying when you're pregnant?"

"I will not go that high," Shiloh will be going higher than me. But I need to stretch my wings because my back has been itching. They want to come out."

"I know, but please be careful."

"I will," I replied. "Now, I am hungry, so let us eat. I warmed up some soup, and we all sat by the fireplace on the couch and ate. When we were done, I cleaned up, and we went outside to sit by the fire pit. Ben lit the logs in the pit, and we sat and enjoyed it. We sat there for a while and reflected on the last few days."

"What do you think Morgan will do when she comes back?" Ben asked.

"I do not think she will do too much; she doesn't have her staff anymore. Of course, she could always find ways to get her staff back. So, we must always be one step ahead of her so she cannot find it."

"Yes, I know."

"Let us get some sleep, Ben; I am so tired.

"You go ahead, Lola; I am not tired yet. Nick wants to hang with me for a while."

"Sure, I am not tired yet either."

"Shiloh, you go ahead too."

"Okay," Lola and Shiloh said as they went to their rooms.

I dropped Shiloh off at her room and then went to my room. I was not as tired as I thought, so I picked up a book and started reading it. I must have dozed off because I didn't even know that Ben had come into the room. When I woke up this morning, I felt terrific. Everything felt light, and nothing bothered me. I went out on the porch and breathed a breath of fresh air. Then, I went back into the house and made me some coffee.

No one in the house was up yet, so I could enjoy my time alone. As everyone started waking up, we planned the day. I wanted to go hiking today. I have not gone hiking for pleasure in a while now.

"Let us go hiking today," I say. "We have not been hiking for pleasure in a while."

"I am all for it," Shiloh said.

So, are we," the guys said.

We ate something for breakfast, and then we all packed up some snacks and water to bring with us on the trails. And piled into Ben's car, then we were on our way to the lakeside trails. It was midafternoon before we were done on the trails, and when we got home, we were wiped out for the rest of the day.

"Ben, I want to fly."

"You know that you are pregnant and can't do that."

"I won't go up high. Maybe just to treetop level."

"Okay, it's against my better judgment, but go ahead and do it. Just be careful."

"I will," I said as I commanded my wings to come out. Shiloh was already in the air. She was flying much higher than me. It was midafternoon before we were done on the trails, and when we got home, we were wiped out for the rest of the day."

"Now I can relax for the rest of the day and do something for myself for once," Lola said. I have wanted to read a complete book, but with everything going on, I could not. I also want to take a long hot bath and relax in the tub. I am going to our room, Ben. Can you bring me dinner to the bedroom tonight?'

'I will bring it in a while."

I went into our room, drew up my bath, and sat down in the water. It felt so good to let the hot water cover my body. It felt like a stream rushing over its rocks. I took a book with me so I could read while I bathed. I got halfway through the book, and I had to get out of the bath because the water was getting cold.

I got out, and Ben was there with dinner. We ate together, and then I sat in my favorite chair in the room and started to read the rest of the book I chose. By the time I read the rest of the book, it was time to go to bed, and I was so tired that I must have gone to sleep.

I must have slept the whole night through. I don't even remember reading the book I had in my hands right now. I woke up feeling refreshed, and I loved that feeling. I have to do this more often. I love being outside in nature. That said, I made myself a cup of coffee and some toast. Then, I went onto the porch and sat in one of the chairs.

I stared out into the air like I could see it. It felt so good to be free of

Morgan, even if it was for a brief time. I know that she will be back. She will come about stronger than before. She might not have her staff, but she is still strong. She has ways to come back anyway. I am not going to worry about that right now. I want to be at peace.

I want to have my baby in peace. I didn't want any fighting with Fae or anyone else, for that matter, so I went back into the house to clean up.

"Shiloh, do you want to go stretch your wings today?" I asked.

"Yeah, I do." She replied.

"Lola, I do not want you flying," Ben said.

"I am not going to; I just want to be in the forest," I replied. "I want Shiloh to go with me. If she went with me, you would not mind so much."

"We will all go if you do not mind," Ben replied.

"I do not mind at all," I said.

We all went into the forest, and Shiloh stretched her wings and started to fly. I, on the other hand, just walked around and studied the plant life and other things. I am fascinated by the plants, trees, and wildlife that live there. I am like a kid in a candy store. I have seen rabbits, frogs, and bugs of all sorts so far. I love looking at the various kinds of trees, too.

There are trees with green moss on them. I love the feel of the moss. It feels like velvet to me. Some of the rocks have moss on them, too. I love being in the forest. It is life to me. When I turned around, I saw that Anuk and Starla were coming through the portal.

"Hey, guys, what's up?" I asked.

"Oh, nothing much; we just heard you rustling around out here and decided to come and see you."

"Well, it's nice to see you guys; how is everything over there in the Fae world?" I asked.

"Everything is good so far; Morgan has been sulking and healing her ego. She still doesn't know that we talk to each other," Starla replied.

"That's good," I wouldn't want her to go off on you and kill you; you guys have been good to us."

"Lola, you are getting big; when will you have your baby?" Starla asked.

"Soon, but not soon enough," I replied.

"Okay, we are going to leave now; it's been nice talking with you," Anuk said. They turned back around and went back through the portal to go back to the Fae world.

"That was nice of them to come and check up on us," Ben said.

"Yeah, it was," I replied, it's nice to know that we have friends on the other side."

"Hey Ben, have you talked to your Maggie yet?" I asked.

"No, I was going to see if I could call her later this afternoon."

"Shiloh, are you ready to get back to the house?" I asked.

"Yes, I am done for the day," She replied.

We all walked back to the house. I stayed out on the porch, though. I just wanted to be outside for a while more. "Ben, can you make me a cup of tea and bring it to me?"

"Yes, I will return with it in a minute," I replied.

"I am in the mood to stay out of here for a while," I say. He returned with my tea and a cup of coffee for himself. He started the fire pit, and we sat by it and relaxed. "I feel so much better with how life is right now," I say.

"I do, too," Ben replied. I am going to be a father, and Nick is going to be an uncle. Everything is on track right now. I cannot wait until the day that our daughter is here. I love that you are growing bigger with our child. You will be a beautiful mother."

"I know I will," I replied. I worry that I cannot keep Summer from harm."

"We all worry about that," Ben said.

"I understand that as well," I said.

"Well, enough of that; I am hungry; I want something, but I don't know what. I looked in the fridge, and nothing appealed to me. Why can't I decide what I want to eat?"

I stand here with the frig open and stare at everything but cannot decide what to eat. I will probably settle on some pickles. I took them out of the frig and put some on a plate and went back into the living room, and sat down again. "I am bored, I say. I need to stretch my wings and fly," I say.

"I know, but you will put the baby at risk," Ben replied.

"I know," I say; I just wish I could go and fly right now. I have read all my books, and I do not have any more right now."

"Well, I guess we will have to get some more," I replied.

"I am ready any time you are; it will give me something to do," I say.

"Let us eat something, and then we can go."

We ate and then drove to the bookstore. I picked up some books, and then we went home. By the time we got home, it was later than I thought. So, I cooked some dinner, and when we were done, I cleaned up the kitchen, then went to my room and started reading one of the books I picked up from the store. Ben came into the room, and we went to bed.

I heard rain tapping, or at least that is what it seemed. I do not know where I am, but I hear a voice calling me from far away. I know that I have listened to that voice from somewhere before. So, I see the person that is calling me. The voice kept calling me and luring me into the forest.

The forest smelled dank and rotting flesh. It was dark, and I could not see anything. Now, I am on edge. As I said, I could not see anything, so I did not know where to go. I just followed the voice. My aunt was there when I got to where the voice originated.

"Auntie, why are you here?" I asked. "You are supposed to be dead."

"I am, dear, but I am here again to warn you that you and your family are in grave danger. Morgan has gathered an army somehow, and she is coming for you.

Then I woke up screaming and told Ben about my dream. We got dressed and went into the kitchen to make something to eat. Shiloh and Nick were already up and in the kitchen.

"What is going on?" Shiloh asked we heard you screaming again."

“We all have to sit down and talk,” I replied. “We have to have a plan to fight Morgan. She has gained an army, and they are coming after us again. I don’t think she’s going to come right away, but I do think that she is waiting for Summer to be born so she can try and take her away from us and train her for the dark side. Last night, my aunt came to me in another dream, warning me about Morgan.”

“That is weird; I had a dream about her last night, too,” Shiloh said.

“Yes, that is the sister’s bond, and the bond is with us and strong,” I replied; we have to produce a plan now that she has forced the situation.

“What can we do?” Shiloh asked.

I shook my head, saying, “I don’t know, but we must produce something.” I replied.

“We only have four people, and we will fight against her and her army of how many.”

“Do not forget we have one unborn child that already knows how to kick some ass. Lola said. Are we going to plan something, or are we going into this blind like the last time?” Lola said.

“We can plan something, but if Morgan decides to surprise us, I doubt it will work as planned,” Ben said.

“We need to train like the last time but harder this time,” Lola says.

“You are not training this time; you must keep your strength up for when Summer comes into this world,” Ben replied.

“I know, I say, but everyone else can train. I will be glad if I can fly again. I miss it. It is like that itch that will not go away. Can I at least go with you and watch you train? I asked. I have not been in the forest since before Morgan came the first time.”

“I know; yes, you may come with us,” Ben replied. Tomorrow morning, we will get up early and do some training; for now, let’s relax for the night. We all sat in the living room by the fireplace for a while.”

“I am going to go read now,” I say. I have not read it in a day or so.”

I went into the bedroom, put on my PJs, and got into bed. I took my book from the nightstand and started to read. I must have dozed off because I did not know that Ben had come in the room and covered me with a blanket, took my book, and put it back on the nightstand. Before I knew it, it was morning and time to eat and go out training.

We ate something quick and had some coffee.

Then we went out to the forest. When we arrived, it was getting cold and overcast, like it would snow again. So, we hurried up our training for the day. Shiloh and Nick fought on the ground because Lola could not fly. Then Nick and Ben fought for a time.

That should be enough for today. Ben said. Anyway, it looks like it is going to storm any minute now. We made it back to the house just in time. It started to snow as soon as we got into the house.

"I hope it is nicer the next time we go out," Lola said. I can't stand feeling like everything is rushed because I love the fresh air of the forest, but damn it makes me tired. I will eat something quick and then head to bed," I told Ben. So, I went to the frig and grabbed some pickles, ate them, and went to the room. I put my PJs on and went to bed.

I must have gone to sleep right away because when I woke up this morning, I felt rested. When I went into the living room, everyone else was up already. How are you ready to go out training today? I asked.

"I am all for it if no one has any objections," Ben said. Nick, Shiloh, are you ready?

"Yeah, sure, why not," They said.

"Okay, let us eat something and get on with it," Ben said.

We ate and had our morning coffee. Then it was time to go. When we got to the clearing in the forest, we started our training right away. Shiloh and Nick began to first.

They went at each other with a vigor I had not seen from them before. Because I would not let Lola fly, we had to do all ground training, and I hope it will be enough.

Then it was mine and Nick's turn to have a go. Nick charged at me like a bull and knocked me over. "Good one, I say; now it is my turn." I did the same, but he was ready for my move. He knocked me to the ground with one blow.

"Shit man. Are you trying to kill me?" I asked.

"Well, Lola said we must train harder," Nick laughed. "Come on, let us go home. We had enough training for today."

"Yeah, I think so, too," I laugh. I am getting hungry also."

We started on our way home, but we had to keep stopping because Lola's legs kept cramping up. She is close to having the baby, and I don't even like her going with us now. But if I said anything, she would only say she was okay and good enough to come. Lola is not one to complain about anything. That is one of the reasons I love her so much. She shows so much strength.

We finally got home; we all were hungry at that point. We had dinner, and Lola went to the bedroom to rest. I went with her to help her put her feet up. Her legs were swollen. I put her to bed, turned off the light, and left the room. I returned to sit by the fireplace and talk to Shiloh and Nick.

"She is close to having the baby," I tell Nick and Shiloh.

"Yeah, I know," they said. Do we have enough training? Nick asked.

"We can only hope that it is enough because this time when Morgan comes, we have no choice but to defeat her. We do not even know when she is coming. It could be a week or a year from now," Ben replied.

As we sat by the fire thinking about what we were going to do to fight Morgan, we heard a scream that came from the bedroom. We all ran to see what was wrong.

"What, what is going on, Lola?" Ben asked.

"I had another dream," Lola said; "Can I talk to Ben alone, please?" I say. "Okay," Nick and Shiloh say as they shut the door.

"Okay, let us hear it," Ben said.

"Morgan has contacted me. She made it clear that we will not know when she is coming. She says that she is coming. She is content with stretching this out. She is toying with us. She also said that she knows when the baby will be born. I know what she wants. She wants to turn Summer to her side because she is immensely powerful. We cannot let that happen. She will destroy the world with that kind of power."

"Morgan will not get to take her; I will protect you and Summer," Ben said. "I am going to go discuss this with Nick and Shiloh. We will produce something to defeat her. Is there anything else that I need to know?" Ben asked.

"Yes, she has her staff back, and I have no idea how she got it back, I replied, "I need to go into the forest so I can go into the Fae world, so I can find out if the others know anything."

"Okay, Lola, but we are all going together. You are almost ready to have the baby. You need to be careful."

"I know; I do not know if the Fae will let you into their world, though."

"Okay, tomorrow morning, all of us will go after we eat something," Ben replied. "Okay, try to get some more rest, Lola. I will talk to Nick and Shiloh about this."

"Okay," I replied.

I went out to talk to Nick and Shiloh. I told them what was happening with Lola's dream. I told them Morgan was toying with us and coming after Summer because she would be extremely powerful. She wants to turn her to the dark side and join her in destroying the world.

Lola also told me that Morgan has her staff back. Lola has yet to learn how she did it. Lola wants to go into the forest to see if the Fae know anything about this.

"I told her that we all will go because she is so close to having the baby," Ben said.

Nick and Shiloh both agreed to go.

"We will be going tomorrow morning after we eat something," Ben said. "Get some rest, guys; something tells me that we are going to have a long day tomorrow. See you tomorrow; I am going to bed."

"See you tomorrow morning," they said.

This morning, we woke up early, ate something, and then left to go into the forest. We reached the forest.

"We need to feel the portal's energy; it should still feel like electric water.

"I found it," Ben shouted. Everyone looked at me.

"Where," Lola asked.

"A couple of feet to the left from where you are standing. I would have fallen through it again. I felt the electric feeling, and that stopped me," Ben replied.

We all went over by Ben and wondered where Ben said the portal was.

"Shiloh, do you want to come with me?" I asked.

"Okay," Shiloh replied.

"I am looking for Starla; she might know about Morgan getting her staff back, including who helped her," I replied. We went through the portal, and we were met with high regard from the Fae. We met with Starla.

"Hey, Starla, I say.

"Hey, what's up, Lola."

"I need to know anything you have on Morgan. She contacted me through my dream the other night. She is coming after my daughter when she gets older. In the meantime, she is satisfied with toying with us until she decides to come."

"Also, I took her staff away from her and put it in a place that I thought she couldn't get it back. But she has, and I do not know how she did it."

"Does any Fae here know any information On Morgan, including how she got her staff back after it has been taken from her and hidden?"

Starlic asked the others that have been gathering.

Only one came up to us and started talking. "The only thing I know about Morgan is that her staff knows her voice, so she only must call on her staff, and it will come to her; you have to destroy it so she cannot get it back." "I am sorry, but that is all I know; I cannot help you more than that."

"Okay, thank you for all your information; it helped a lot," I say. "We must go back to our world now."

"I want to see the baby when you have a chance," Starlic said before we left.

"I will bring her when I can. I replied. See you soon." "Wait, does that mean I can enter the Fae world whenever possible?" I asked.

"Yes," Starla said.

"Thank you, that makes me so happy," I say.

"I thought it would," Starla replied.

We went back through the portal. When we returned, Ben and Nick were still sitting on a rock, and they asked what we found out.

"Well, we discovered that Morgan can call her staff, and it will come to her. Unfortunately, that is all we found out. It did help, though, because we now know that we must destroy the staff so she cannot use it. When it comes time and she comes to take Summer, we must focus on destroying her staff."

“Okay, that is a good thing to hear,” Ben said. “Now we can work around that information.”

Yes, now I must deal with her playing with my head. Let’s go home. Oh, Starlic wants to see Summer when I get to go with her to see the Fae.”

“Who is Starlic again?” Ben asked.

“She is Anuk’s assistant; remember we met her in the forest when they came out of the portal with Anuk.”

“Oh, that’s right.”

“After I have our baby, I will have to train eventually. I said to Ben. I hope sooner than later. You know that I have been itching to fly again.”

“I know, Ben said. But you must make sure you are up to it. You will be of no use to anyone if you are injured.”

I cannot wait until this is all over. We must get her staff away from her to destroy it, and we have to be careful. If I learned one thing from Morgan, she is unpredictable. You think that you have her one minute, and she shows you that you do not in the next minute.”

“That is for sure,” Ben replied. For now, do not worry about anything. It would be best if you had your strength. Right, get some rest. I will bring some food to the room for you in a little while.”

Chapter 20

Okay, I said and went to our room. I have been so tired lately that I just lay down and sleep. I must have fallen asleep because I did not feel or hear Ben enter the room. He was there when I woke up this morning and woke up shortly after I did.

Ben, I need you to stay around for the next few days. Summer is coming either today or tomorrow. I am starting to get crampy, and that means that she is coming soon.

"Okay," I say.

We went out into the living room and sat down on the couch by the fireplace. Then Ben went to make me a cup of tea and some toast. I ate it in silence.

"Nick, if you and Shiloh want to train later, you must go by yourselves."

Okay, Nick said. We will stick around because you may need some help once Lola goes into labor.

Okay, Ben and Lola replied.

Ben, I will return to our room; I feel bad.

Okay, I will come in and check on you in a while.

Okay, I replied.

Nick, Shiloh, it's been a while since she entered the bedroom; I will check on her now.

Okay, Let us know if you need us for anything.

I will, I replied as I left the room.

Lola, how are you feeling? Ben asked.

I am good, but she is coming soon. I am in more pain than earlier.

Okay, I will watch you as the night goes on. Do you want anything? I asked her.

Yes, Can I have some water, please?

I will bring it in.

Thank you,

You're welcome, I said as I left the room.

Well, how is she doing? Nick and Shiloh asked.

She is getting closer, but she is good. She asked me for water.

Ben came in with the water that I asked for. I sipped on it and said thanks. I am close now. She is coming soon. Gather some towels, some warm water, and something for me to bite down on.

Okay, Ben said. I will also get Nick and Shiloh to help too. I went to get the things that Lola requested. I also asked Nick and Shiloh to go in with her. It is time.

"Nick, can you please call her doctor?" Let him know to be on standby.

"Sure," I say as I pick up my phone.

We went in with Lola and sat with her while Ben was gathering the things that he needed.

Nick finds Ben and helps him gather things. Lola said. "I am going into labor now."

Okay, Nick said. He then left the room. Ben, where are you? I called out.

I am right here! Ben said. What are you yelling?

Lola is in labor, so get your shit together. I said.

Well, are you going to help me get everything together, or are you just going to stand there? I asked him.

Okay, please give me something to do then. Nick said.

Here, grab these bowls, get some warm water, and take them to the bedroom. Ben said.

Okay, Nick said.

I will be there in a minute. Ben said.

Hurry up, Nick said.

I will, Ben said. Tell Lola I will be there in a minute; I must get the towels.

I am here, now what do I do?

For one, you keep the water warm, not hot. Lola said. Shiloh, you can keep wiping my forehead off from sweating. Ben, be here by my side. When it is time to push, someone must catch the baby. That means you have been between my legs. Nick, will you do it?

Yes, Nick said. I will be there to guide her out. Is that okay with you, Ben?

Yes, Ben said.

Nick, find a chair and sit at the bottom of my feet. Lola said.

I went to find a chair and did what Lola asked of me. I sat by her feet, just waiting for something to happen.

Lola's face screwed up in pain as another contraction hit her.

Count backward from five to one. Ben said.

It is okay now; it has passed, Lola said as Shiloh wiped the sweat from my forehead. Ben, can you get me some ice, please? Lola asked.

I left the room to get her the ice and quickly returned to the room just as she started to push. She let out a scream and pushed.

Ben, you can call the doctor now. She is coming now.

I called the doctor and asked her to come, and that Lola was in labor now. Thank God she only lives down the street from us. She made it here in no time.

Okay, I am here. The doctor said. Nick, you can go to Lola's side now. Let us see what is going on down here, Shall we? She is here. Just push when I tell you to. Lola's face screwed up in pain as another contraction hit her. Push Lola, the doctor said. They began to count, one, two, three, and stop pushing. That is good, Lola.

How is it going? Ben asked.

She is doing well. The doctor told me.

Another contraction hit her, and the doctor told her to push. The doctor counted again. One, two, three, and stop, good. On your next contraction, try as hard as you can. They will be your last push.

"Okay, here we go the doctor said as a contraction hit Lola. Push as hard as you can.

Lola pushed, and the baby slid into the doctor's hands. The doctor cleaned up the baby and laid her in Lola's arms. Do you want to cut the cord? The doctor asked Ben.

Yes, Ben said. Then, I took the scissors and cut it.

I will tie it off. The doctor said. Let us get her dressed and warm. Do you have a name for her yet?

Yes, Lola said. Her name is Summer.

Well, Summer, you are home. The doctor said. She started to cry. Okay, my job here is done. If you need anything, give me a call, okay?

I will have plenty of questions. Lola said. I will be calling.

Oh, I am sure you will. The doctor said. For now, get your rest and get your strength back. Ben, will you walk me out? The doctor asked.

Sure, Ben said.

Make sure Lola gets enough rest. I know how she can get it. She is so stubborn, but she must rest for herself and the baby.

Okay, I will make sure that she gets enough rest. I saw the doctor outside and then returned to the room where Lola and everyone else were. Nick, Shiloh, let us leave her to rest for a while. Lola, I will check on you in a bit.

Okay, she said in a sleepy voice.

I left her to rest and went to talk to Nick and Shiloh. Let us celebrate; who wants a drink? I asked.

I will have whatever you are having. Nick said.

I will have a beer. Shiloh said. I am glad that I was here for Lola. She said.

Me too, Nick said.

I am glad you were here, too. I say with a sigh. I could not have done this without you. I went in to check on Lola and Summer. They were sleeping and snuggling with each other. It was so beautiful that it warmed my heart. God, I love this woman and our child. I will do anything for them.

Well, how are they? Nick and Shiloh asked.

They are sleeping. I say. They are so cute together. I will put Summer in her crib so Lola can rest better. I entered our room, took Summer, and put her in her crib. Lola moved but did not wake up. I left the room, returned to the living room, and sat on the couch by the fireplace.

Shiloh.

Yes.

Can you make some coffee, please? Ben asked. I want to talk to Nick alone for a minute.

Okay, Shiloh said.

Nick, we must start training again soon. He said.

I know, Nick said. When do you want to start? Nick asked.

Let's give it a month so we all can bond with Summer. I reply.

Agreed, Nick says. I, for one, want to bond with Summer. I have always wanted you to be happy, Ben. Whatever you may think, that is all I ever wanted. I know I have done some shitty shit in my life, but I am here for you now.

I know Nick, and I am glad that you are here with us. You had to learn hard lessons, and I realize that now. Nick started to cry.

Please do not cry, Nick, I say.

I can't help it, Ben; I have not thanked you enough. If we had not been forced back together, we would not be here today. At the same time, if I were not here, you would not be in this mess.

Do not worry about it, I replied. If you learn from your mistakes, it's all good. Shiloh came back into the room with two cups of coffee.

Here you go, two cups of hot coffee. Shiloh says.

Ben?

Yes, Shiloh.

Please let me know when Lola is awake. I want to talk to her.

Yes, Shiloh.

Thank you.

Shiloh?

Yes, Nick.

I just got done talking to Ben, He said.

Okay, Shiloh said. Thanks for letting me know. I will say the same things or something similar when I talk to Lola.

Shiloh?

Yes, Nick.

How did you know what I talked to Ben about?

Did you forget that I can hear your thoughts? Shiloh asked.

Um, yes, Nick said.

Well, there you go, that is your answer. Shiloh said, laughing.

Oh, you, Nick said as he threw a pillow at her.

Guys, I am going to check on Lola. Ben said.

Okay, they said.

I went into our room and saw that Lola was awake. How are you feeling? I asked her.

Surprisingly good. She said.

Are you up for talking? Ben asked. Shiloh wants to come in and speak to you.

Yes, I feel up to it. I say. Send her in when you go out.

Okay, I am going to let her know now.

Okay, Lola said.

Shiloh, Ben called out.

Yes, Ben.

You can go in and talk to Lola now. Ben said.

Thank you, Shiloh said. Then I went to see Lola.

Hey, Lola.

Hey, what's up, Shiloh? Lola asked.

I wanted to talk to you about something. Shiloh said.

Okay, Shoot.

Well, Shiloh said.

Out with it, Shiloh. Lola said.

I did not know about you, I say, and if I had, I would not have gone along with Morgan's plan. She didn't tell me about any of what she was planning. I feel bad about what she did to your aunt. I hate that she was going to do the same to you.

Shiloh, I am not blaming you for what Morgan has done. Lola said.

I know, but she used me to get to you, and that is what I am fighting against. Now we have a little one to protect, and when she gets older, I hope she doesn't think badly of me.

When it is time, we will tell her what has happened, and you did not know what you were doing, I say. We will make sure that she knows that Morgan manipulated you into doing what she wanted you to do. Do not worry, Shiloh, she will understand.

I love you, Lola.

I love you too, Shiloh; now come over here so I can hug you.

I went over to hug her big sister. Crying, I said I love you, Lola.

I will go and let you rest now.

Okay, I replied. I will see you later.

I left her room and returned to sit with the guys in the living room. I need a stiff drink. I said.

You do not drink anything harder than a glass of wine occasionally. Nick said.

I know, Shiloh said. But I want to get drunk and go to bed. The last couple of days have been long and daunting for me.

Nick, can you make me a drink and bring it to me in our room? She asked.

"Sure," I replied.

I am going to get ready for bed," I say as I leave them and go to the bedroom.

Man, what is it with women? They are all so emotional. Nick said.

Are you asking me? I am going to check on Lola. I left to check on her. She was sleeping, and Summer was next to her, just cooing away. I took Summer and held her, and played with her for a while.

You know, you are so cute. I say to her. Do you want to see Uncle Nick? I speak. She gives me a great big smile as an answer. Okay, let us go then, I say with a smile.

Hey Nick, someone wants to see you.

Oh yes, who is that? He said.

Ms. Summer wants to see you.

Let me take Shiloh her drink, and I will be right back out. Nick said.

Okay, I will play with her until you come back out. I told him.

Okay, I said.

Nick came back out from giving Shiloh her drink. "Okay, give me that little one. I cannot wait to hold her and play with her. I hope to be as good a father as you are, Ben, someday."

Nick, you will be a great father when that time comes.

I know I will; it is just a fear of mine. I say. For now, I want to play with this baby.

I hear a knock at the door, and I turn to Nick. Does anyone know that we are here? I do not think so, I said.

I cautiously go to the door and say, who is it?

It is me, Starla; Anuk sent me, the voice said.

I opened the door and asked, "What are you doing here, and why do you look so different?

I am here because I have important information to talk to Lola about. I look different because when I am in the mundane world, I must look human so I do not stand out in the crowd. Humans aren't used to seeing beings with wings in their world. I must dress to fit in here, and I wouldn't say I like it.

I let her in and talked to her for a few minutes. Then I went to see if Lola was up to having guests.

Lola, I called. Starlic is here to see you. Do you feel up to talking with her?

Yes, send her in, please. She said.

Starlic, do you mind if I stay here with you? I asked.

Sure, I have nothing to hide, she said as she entered the room.

Why have you come to see me? Lola asked.

I have valuable information for you. She said. The first thing is, how are you doing? She asked.

You know that I heal quickly because of the Fae in me. Lola said.

That is what I am here to talk to you about. Starlic said. You not only have Fae in you.

What do you mean? Lola asked.

I have been digging into your lineage and found that you also have some elven.

Holy Shit, now way. Lola said.

I can tell that it is shocking to you.

Well, yes, it is shocking. Lola said. Okay, start from the beginning.

"Okay, Starlic said. Well, I decided to keep digging, and I found that someone on your father's side of the family had married into the elven line.

Chapter 21

Just to let you know, I have no idea where or when this happened because they are either dead or they do not want to be found. I can't find any of these people anywhere.

Okay then. What else is there? I have this feeling that there is more.

That is another thing. Starlic said. Your elven line is one of many things we have to worry about. Morgan found out, and now she is wreaking havoc in both the mundane and the magical world. She went nuts when she found out about the elven in you. We are going to have to work together on fighting her.

Do you know when she is coming after us? I asked.

No, that is the thing. I cannot read her mind. She has blocked everyone from reading. Starlic said. It could be tomorrow or five months from now. There is so much at stake now. The entire world is counting on us.

What should I do? Lola asked.

We better do something soon. Starlic said. I will return to the magical realm and see if I can gather as many people as possible. I will come back and report to them.

Well, I do not know anyone here on the mundane plain. So, it is just us here. Lola said.

I will see who I can get together with. Ben said. I have a few people that will help, but I am sure someone will. I will wait for you to report back here, though, before I go. I need to know how many people you have, and I do not want to leave Lola unprotected.

"Okay, Starlic said. I will leave you now. I go back to the portal and go through, and I am back in the magical world. I start talking to the other Fairies and Elves to gather and plan something about Morgan. I spoke to the head elf, Floos, and asked him to gather as many elves as he could after I explained the situation to him.

Floos went about his business, gathering as many as he could. He gathered about one hundred elves, and I gathered about as many Fairies. Floos and I met with all the Fairies and elves and reported to Lola and Ben. "Okay, we have one hundred elves and one hundred Fairies.

That is going to be good enough. Lola said.

Okay, Ben said. I now have to go to Los Angeles to see if I can get anyone to help us. I already called my family, and they are in for the fight.

No, Ben, it would be best if you didn't go; Morgan will kill you. Lola cried.

I have to try, Ben said. We need as many as we can get. I will be careful. Nick Shiloh, will you take care of Lola and the Summer for me?

Yes, we will.

Starla, I need a few people from the magical world to protect them as well.

Will do, Starla said. I will have five Fairies and five elves here around the clock.

Thank you, Ben said. I go and pack my bags for the trip to LA. I get a terrible feeling that something is not right. I do not think about it much. I do not have time for this right now. I go and eat something and get on my way.

Starla had ten people guarding me. Nick and Shiloh tried to keep my mind off Ben leaving. I know he has to do this, but I wouldn't say I like it. LA is a dangerous place for him to go right now. I had told Ben to call me when he got to the hotel. I was playing with Summer when the phone rang.

Hey, it is me. Ben said. I made it okay.

Thank God, I say with a sigh. I was playing with Summer when you called.

How is everything up there? Ben asked.

Everything is good. I replied. I am well protected.

Good, I was letting you know that I am okay. I will head to my office and talk to everyone there to see if I can get them on board.

Okay, Be careful, Ben. I love you.

I will; I love you too. I unpacked my clothes because I will stay in LA for two days. I went to my office and gathered around for an emergency meeting. I explained what was happening, and everyone there was on board. We had to tie some things up at the office, and then we will close for some time.

Everyone went home early, packed some clothes, and met me the next day in the parking lot of the office. We are going to stay here for the night, and we will leave in the morning to go up north.

You must follow me because none of you have been where I am staying. So, stay close and don't stray from the route. We will all stop to eat together.

We cleaned the office, so we didn't have to do it in the morning. I called Lola and told her that I would be coming back tomorrow instead of the next day. I will have the people from the office producing me.

How many are there? Lola asked. I need to make room for them.

About thirteen, I say.

Okay, she said. I will make room for them.

Okay, I will call her before I leave in the morning. Have a good night, Lola.

I went to bed, but every time I closed my eyes, I felt uneasy. Like someone was watching me, I will not get that much sleep tonight. I just got to sleep, and my alarm went off to let me know it was time to get up. So, we all got up, locked up the building, and left town to go up north. I called Lola to tell her that we left and that I would call her when we all got into town. "I can't wait to see you, Lola.

While driving, I still could not shake the feeling that someone was watching me. I will be glad to get home. Getting closer and closer to what I call home for now, the sense of someone watching me kept getting stronger. I remember thinking, I cannot wait until all this is over. Then, I did not have time to think about anything else because my tire blew. I had to make sure that I could control my car. Thank God everyone behind me was watching because there would have been a bad accident.

All the guys from my office stopped and helped me change my tire, and we were on our way again.

"how in the hell did this happen?" The guys asked.

"I have a sneaking suspicion that it was Morgan. She wants me to make it to the house after she gets there herself.

"So, get there before she does, just to piss her off," They say. I hear when the enemy is pissed off, they make mistakes.

We finally made it to the house. Now I can breathe a little easier. Lola ran out the door, jumped on me, hugged me, and kissed me hard.

I missed you so much.

I missed you too, Lola. We have company, though. She blushed and got down from hugging me.

Come on in, guys. Ben told me you were coming, and I made plenty of room for you. I will make some coffee and food, and we can relax for the night. We can discuss what we can do tomorrow. I went into the kitchen and got to work. Ben came in after me.

I cannot wait to get you alone tonight, Lola. Ben said in that low, sexy voice that I could not resist.

Why is that? She teased.

Because I am going to bend you over the bed and tie you up and make you come hard, I heard her gasp, and then she hit me playfully.

Ben, you are such a perv. You know we have company.

You know that does not mean anything to me; I missed you. Oh, and get your vibe ready. I plan to use it tonight. I want you to be screaming and begging tonight. I left the kitchen. Leaving her to ponder on what I said. She blushed. I love it when she blushes. It gave her enough time to cool down before she came out to serve our guests.

Lola came out of the kitchen with the food and coffee. She gave everyone their food before she served herself. Then she sat down with the rest of us by the fireplace. She was talking to us as we sat and ate. When everyone was finished, she took the plates into the kitchen, washed them, and put them away. When she was done, she showed everyone their rooms to sleep in and then went into the bedroom herself. I followed her because I was also tired.

Lola, you are not going to sleep yet. I asked. Remember what I said to you earlier?

Yes, she said.

Yes, what? I asked her.

Yes sir.

That is better, I told her. Now get undressed; I want you sweating, panting, and screaming my name. She did as she was told, but she undressed slowly so I could ravish her with my eyes.

When she was done, I told her to bend over the bed. "I am going to tie you to the bedpost now," I noticed her vibe was sitting on the bed beside her. That is a good girl; you remembered I asked you to bring out your vibe.

Chapter 22

Now I am going to pet your sweet wet pussy with it.

How do you know that I am wet for you? She asked teasingly.

Oh, baby, I know your body and its reaction to what I do to you. Besides that, I can smell you. I started to stroke her pussy with her vibe, and she moaned.

That is a girl, Moan, for me. She moaned again. I took the vibe away just then, and she moaned and said, please do not stop.

She, baby, I am not stopping; I am switching what I am doing. I gave her a swat on her ass, and she bucked forward and moaned.

Do you want another one? I asked. She did not answer, so I gave her another swat. She moaned louder. Every time I gave her a swat, her moans got louder and louder.

Do you like that? I asked.

Yeeeeesssss.

God, Lola, I am so hard for you.

I kept switching between rubbing with her vibe and smacking her ass until I was satisfied that she had enough. I slipped my hand between her legs and rubbed her with her vibe.

Fuck me, baby, you are so wet. I stopped rubbing her and planted my face between her legs. Now I want to taste you. I started licking and sucking her until she came with a scream. I let her calm down, and then I started again. This time I started rubbing her clit with my fingers. When she was moaning again, I took my hand away. I quickly undressed because I was about to explode. I drove into her dripping wet pussy and fucked her so hard she screamed again from the sheer force of me pushing into her. I could not hold myself back anymore, and I exploded with the might of a Viking.

By the time we were done, we were both drenched with sweat and panting and trying to control our breath. We curled up next to each other and went to sleep. The following day, when we woke up, we were still cuddled up together.

It is time to get up. Lola said.

I know. Be said, I do not want to.

I do not want to either, but we have guests.

Come on, sleepy head. Get up. Lola said.

Okay, okay he said.

We must face the day and determine what we will do about Morgan. Ben said. I will be out soon, okay?

Okay, I say.

Fuck Me, Ben, you made me so sore I cannot walk.

That was the point. He said with a chuckle.

I am going to take a shower, and I will be out. Then you can take your and be done with it. Then I will cook breakfast then.

Okay, Ben said.

I took my shower and got dressed. Then I went out to tell Ben That I was done. He went to shower, and I started to make breakfast for everyone.

When he was done, he came back out.

How do you feel, Lola?

Besides not being able to walk without pain, I am fine.

He just gave me one of his halves, smiled, and continued his business. I served everyone their food and then served myself. I sat down with my food and enjoyed everyone's company. It is nice to have a whole house of people again. The following people who showed up were Ben's family. I loved seeing his sister again. I missed her. I miss talking to her because she always listened to me instead of criticizing me.

Hey, Sis, Ben said.

Hey, Ben, she said. What is going on?

Oh, you know, saving the world again. Morgan is up to her evil deeds again.

That'sThat's all; what else is new when it comes to her?

Here, sit down and have something to eat. I said.

Thank you, Ben. I would love to. After I eat, I need some rest. I drove a long way to get here.

I know; I will have Lola set you up.

Okay, she said.

Where is the rest of the family? I asked.

They will be here in a couple of days. She said.

Okay, I said.

When everyone was done eating, Lola took the dishes and washed everything. Then, she showed Maggie to her room, where she would sleep.

I missed you.

I missed you too, Maggie replied.

I hate having to call you in these circumstances, but Morgan is after us again, and we need as many people as we can get.

I know, do not worry about it. It gave me an excuse to see my niece.

You know, you do not need an excuse to come here. You are welcome here any time that you want to come. I gave her a great big hug and left her to be so she could get some sleep. But, before I left, I told her we would talk tomorrow.

Okay, I replied.

I went to my room, and Ben was already there. Everyone is settled for the night," I asked.

Yes, Man, I am so stressed out, I can hardly stand it, Ben replied.

Here, let me see if I can help. She said.

She started to rub my shoulders, and then she went lower. Then she got out of bed, stood before me, and undressed.

Ben, get undressed for me.

I did what she asked. Then she bent between my legs and took my cock into her mouth. She sucks hungrily. I was at the breaking point, and she stopped.

Why did you stop? I asked.

Because I want you to be fucking you when you come. I planted myself firmly on his Cock and began to ride him. I came at the same time that he did. When we were done, we were both drenched with sweat and panting.

How did you like it? I asked.

I loved it, Lola. You know, sometimes you just blow my fucking mind.

I am glad that you liked it. I say. Then, I got back on the bed, and Ben came up beside me, and we went to sleep. When we woke up the next day, it was in the afternoon.

Wow, we slept the whole night. I am surprised. He said.

Good afternoon, Lola.

Good afternoon, Ben. I love you.

I love you too, Lola.

As the day starts, everyone is on edge. Morgan has wreaked havoc on the mundane and the magical worlds, and we must stop her somehow.

How are we going to defeat Morgan? Lola asks.

I don't know, Ben said. But the first thing we should do is train. We have to be fast thinking and moving. We must be able to move around so fast she can't see us.

Okay, can we start tomorrow? Lola asked. I want to spend some time with everyone here.

Yes, Lola, Ben said.

Let us all go hiking today and not worry about anything else.

We can do that. Ben said. Is anybody up for hiking today?

Yes, where are we going?

Well, Lola and I have been hiking in the forest to this clearing in the middle of a mountain. It is a few miles up, so I hope you have good hiking shoes.

We do, everyone said at once.

All right, let us eat, and then we can be on our way.

Yes, let us do that. We are hungry.

So, we all ate something and then got ready to go. We packed some water and snacks and then went to the forest. It took us a while to get up to the clearing because Lola had not been hiking in a time because of being pregnant. Also, she was carrying Summer on her back. But, when we finally reached it, it was so beautiful.

This is also where we will train, so get used to it.

Sure thing, boss, everyone said.

Starting tomorrow, we will start coming up here every day for training.

That said, we sat down to rest for a while, ate some snacks, and took in the view before we decided to go back down the mountain. By the time we got back to the house, we were exhausted. We did not even want to do anything, so we just had the rest of the snacks and had some coffee. Then, I went to bed.

Ben and I must have the whole night through because we woke up this morning refreshed, a little sore but refreshed.

God, I am famished. Lola said.

I am, too, Ben said. Let's eat something before we go to train.

Yes, let's do that.

I went out into the kitchen and cooked breakfast and served everyone before I served myself. When everyone was done eating, I took the dishes, washed them, and put them away. Then Ben and I got ready to hike the mountain to train.

Is everyone ready to train today?

Not really, but we have no choice in the matter at this point.

Well, for what are you waiting? Get ready to go. Pack snacks and water; you are going to need them today. Chop, chop, let's get going. We started our hike up the mountain, and when we got to the clearing, we all sat to rest for a few minutes.

Okay, enough, let's get training, Shiloh, let's get up in the air, I say.

Okay, Shiloh said as she extended her wings, and then she was up in the sky. I followed her.

Wait a minute, what just happened? One of the guys from my office asked.

I forgot to tell you. Ben said. Lola found out that she is a halfling. And just a few days ago, she found some elf in her blood, too.

What is a halfling? He said.

It is a person that has fairy blood, Ben explained. Her mother was from the magical world, and Shiloh, her sister, is all Fae.

I cannot believe what I am seeing. He said. What about this Morgan person?

She is Lola's and Shiloh'sShiloh's grandmother and the Fae queen. I say. She is evil as hell. Enough explaining; we should get to the training now.

Okay, what do you want me to do?

Do you know how to spar? I asked him.

Yes, he said.

Okay, I said. We can start with that, then.

Does everyone here know how to spar? I asked.

Yes, everyone said.

So, get to it. I say.

Okay, boss, whatever you say. They started to go at it.

I turned to the guy that I was sparing with and told him to lunge at me and try to move around me before I flipped him over my shoulder.

I charged at him, but I was not fast enough, and he flipped me.

You must be better than that; show me everything you've got. Remember, don't hold back. Also, don't show any weakness; Morgan will chew you up and spit you out. I charged at him again, and this time, I didn't-didn't hold anything back. I knocked him over and knocked the wind out of him.

"Is that what you mean by not holding back?

Yes, now you get it. Now, let's try it again. Show me everything that you have. Remember, do not hold back.

Let's start the real sparing now. I am going to charge you. Please do the same thing, but try to flip me now. I gave him no warning and charged. He had little time to think.

On instinct, I posed to flip him, and when it came time, I did flip him.

Good, I say. Now, let's try to knock each other down using our hands and arms and wrestle.

Okay, He said.

I grabbed Ben with all my might and tossed him on the ground.

How is that, I say.

Good, he says. Now I am going to do the same thing to you. I went to grab the guy, and he moved past me. So, I grabbed him from behind and tossed him to the ground.

Don't turn your back on the enemy. I say. They will always get you. Okay, let's rest while we wait for the girls to finish.

Okay, he said.

When the girls were done, we headed back down the mountain to the house.

I am so exhausted that I cannot keep my eyes open. Ben, can you make dinner tonight? She asked.

No, if you want to go to our room to rest, go ahead. Ben said. I will bring food to you when I am done.

Thank you. Can you bring me a drink, please?

Yes, I will be in a bit with everything.

I left to go to the bedroom to rest; I put Summer in her crib and laid on the bed. I must have fallen asleep because when I woke up to go to the bathroom, I saw a glass of water on my nightstand and Ben sleeping beside me. When Ben and I woke in the morning, we were both sore as hell from the training the previous day.

Do we have to go to training today? Lola asked.

No, we do not have to go today. I say. Every other day for training will be fine. I will let the others know. I went into the living room to let the others know, but no one was up yet. So, I just waited. What else could I do? I made breakfast for Lola and me because No one else was up. Lola came out of the bedroom.

Go back into the room, Lola. I will bring breakfast to you today.

Okay, I replied, then left the kitchen.

I take a tray loaded with grapes and cheese into our room and set it down on the bed. She started to take some grapes, and I stopped her.

Why did you stop me?

Because I want to feed you.

Okay, I said, looking at him. You know, sometimes when you are in the room, you take my breath away. I love you so much.

Chapter 23

I love you too, Lola.

When Ben and I were done eating, we heard the gang in the dining room. Everyone was starting to get up. Rest today, Lola. I will bring you anything you want today. Read a book I know that you last read a while ago.

You do not have to tell me twice. She said. I am grateful for this time.

I went out into the living room and told everyone that we were not going to train today. We do not have to train every day. Every other day will suffice. Lola and I already had our breakfast, so that I will cook for all of you now. I will call you when I am done cooking. Everything will be buffet style so you can serve yourselves.

After cooking everything, I arranged it so they could serve themselves. Then, I went to check on Lola and to see if she needed anything.

Do you need anything? I asked her.

Yes, please pour me a glass of wine and bring it to me.

Yes, I will be back in a minute.

I poured Lola's wine, then took it to her. She was still reading when I went to give it to her.

Are you having a fun time relaxing and reading?

Yes, I am. It is a much-needed time. I have not read in so long I forgot what books looked like.

Good, tomorrow we have to train, and we will focus on you and Shiloh.

Okay, I will have some dinner when you get it done.

Okay, dinner will be done in about an hour. I will bring you some food then.

Okay, in the meantime, I am going to play with summer. She just woke up from her nap. Ben left the room and went to cook dinner for everyone. I picked my baby girl up and started playing with her.

Mama, Summer said, and I started to cry because she said her first word just now. Oh, my baby girl. You started talking.

I am so proud of you. Ben came in with a plate of food for us. Summer turned around and said DaDa and Ben almost dropped the plate.

She called me DaDa, He said.

Yes, she started talking a few minutes ago when she called me Mamma.

Oh my god, he started to cry. My baby started to talk. When Lola and I were done eating, we played with summer for a while. I took our dishes to the kitchen and put them in the sink. Then, I assumed everyone else's plates and washed the dishes. I told everyone that I was turning in early for the night and left to go to the bedroom to the bedroom and play with Summer some more. I saw that she was getting tired, so I put her down to bed.

Lola, I suggest we get some sleep too. It is going to be a long day tomorrow.

Is your Maggie going to take care of summer for us? I do not want to take her with us now that she is walking. I am afraid that she will go missing.

I will ask her in the morning. I think she will, though. She has been wanting to see her for a while now.

Okay, I said. For now, let's get some sleep. We got into bed, curled up beside each other, and slept. I must have been having a dream. It felt so real, though, like I was there.

I was lured out of the house by a voice calling my name. It sounded like my mother, but something was off. I was drawn to a cliff in the woods. The voice told me to jump, and you will be with me forever. No, I say. This is not what my mother would have wanted. I have a family now. I have a beautiful husband and baby to take care of now. I know, the voice said. But I am here to take you with me. No! I shouted. Just jump, will you? The voice spoke again. Then Morgan revealed her proper form. I knew something was off at that moment.

I woke up screaming in my bed. Then Ben woke up.

What! What happened?

Morgan is coming. Damn, that woman, she is always in my head. She was here last night. At first, I thought that she was my mother, but something was off. She had me on a cliff in the woods. She was trying to get me to jump. I kept telling her no. Then, she revealed herself to me at the end of the dream.

How long do we have? Ben asked.

One or two days.

Okay, let's get the crew up. We have to train as early as possible today.

Lola and I went to wake everyone up and tell them the situation. Everyone ate something, and then we packed snacks and water. We are going to have to work hard today. Lola told me we only have one or two days until Morgan comes for us.

Holy shit! The crew exclaimed. How and the fuck are we going to be ready in that small of time? They asked.

Well, we are going to have to do with what we have. I know we don't have much time, but if we train well today. We will have it in the bag. Lola and I and the crew left to hike up the mountain to the clearing where we always train.

Today, I will leave you to it to concentrate on Lola and Shiloh.

Okay, they went to work, and I went to Lola and Shiloh.

Okay, girls, let us get going on your training. I said. Get up in the air.

Okay, they say.

"I will go first, Shiloh said. She was off the ground before I knew it. She did not even give me a chance to respond before she was off. I followed her.

You are always first, I complained. I want to be first sometime.

Well, you have to act faster than me then, and we both laughed.

Then we went at it. She came at me, and I went after her. We fought and fought until we could not fight anymore and out of breath. I am not going into detail because it was the same moves that we have made before. We came down to rest and eat something before returning to the mountain.

We were all dirty, sweaty, and ready to go home for the night. After we ate, we started on our way back to the house.

Chapter 24

When we got back home, we were all tired and wanted nothing but our beds. I was not hungry, so I just poured myself some wine and went into the bedroom. Ben said good night and followed me to the room.

I drank my wine, and then Ben and I went to sleep. It was about 6.00 a.m. when I woke up with a start. I know the time because I looked at the clock on my nightstand when I woke up. I woke Ben up. She is here.

What?

Morgan is here, close by.

Okay, let us get everyone up.

Lola and I started waking everyone up, one by one, and telling them to meet in the living room. We told them that Morgan was close by and we must get ready for the fight.

There is no time to reflect, I said. Some of us will not make it through this, but let me say how much I appreciate everyone for helping us through this time of need. We also have help for the Elven people in the magical world. They will be here in a couple of minutes.

Where is Summer? I asked.

Maggie has her.

Good, it is good that I do not have to worry about that.

Yes, it is good. Ben said. I don't know what I would do if something happened to her.

Okay, the Elven people are here. We need to talk to them. I went outside to greet them. I let them know that we needed as much distraction as possible.

We are good with that.

All I need is for you to run around her as much as you can and keep it that way so we can fight her. This time, we plan to put her somewhere so that she can't cause any more harm to anyone else.

Okay, we will do that.

Suddenly, Lola came running out of the house shouting (she is here; Morgan is here).

Everyone took their places and stood their stance.

Let us try to do this with minimal bloodshed, shall we? Ben said.

Okay, boss, the troops said in unison.

Morgan came up the driveway, not noticing how many people we had. When she finally notices, I see the fear creep into her eyes momentarily. She will never let anyone know that she is in fear.

Well, well, what do we have here?

A small army. Lola said. I do not want to fight you, but you give me no choice.

Everyone attacks! Lola shouted. We have to get her staff away from her.

Then everyone started to charge at Morgan, and she was knocked to the ground.

While some of the elves pursued her with knives and swords in an attempt to stab her, The other elves ran around her in several directions to confuse her. All the others went after knives and swords, impaling her. She suffered some cuts and knife wounds, but they weren't severe enough to prevent her from continuing with the fight.

In the end, we were successful in taking Morgan's staff away from her and using some spells to bind her. We carried her to the top of a mountain and located a suitable hiding place for her there. Before we sealed the cavern entrance, Lola told Morgan she was taking over the thrown and running things as they should be.

After that, we sealed her in with her very own staff. Then, we shattered the team into several pieces and hid them in different places so they couldn't be found. When we finally got back to the house, we were filthy, hot, and covered in blood and repulsed by what they had been forced to do. However, they knew Morgan had not given them any other choice.

After expressing their gratitude, the elves departed for their home in the magical world. Ben looked around at the other group members and said, "Well, that was intense."

"I hope we never have to do that again," Lola said.

"Me too," Ben replied, taking a few deep breaths." We did what had to be done to make things right.

A voice halted the gathering just as they were taking a moment to regain their breath and said, "What happened here?"

We all turn around simultaneously to find a person standing at the edge of the driveway. The stranger had a pleasant appearance, with soft eyes that seemed to take in all that was happening around them. Ben took a step forward while maintaining a wary eye on the newcomer. "Who are you?"

The unfamiliar person gave a friendly smile. "Hello there, my name is Aiden." I happened to be walking by at the time, and I witnessed the commotion. "Is there anything that I can do to assist you in this matter?"

“We just had taken care of the situation just before you got here; there’s nothing you need to worry about,” Lola said while trying to catch her breath.

Aiden nodded, aware of the group’s requirement for confidentiality. “I see. I am just passing through, but if there’s anything I can do to help, please don’t hesitate to contact me. I will be camping in the woods not too far from here in a clearing that I found.

When glancing at Aiden, I got the feeling that he was trustworthy. “Thank you, Aiden. “We are grateful for the offer, but at this point, I believe we have everything under control,” Lola said.

Aiden continued to smile and said, “All right then. Take care, and don’t put yourself in danger.” Then he turned and walked away. After losing sight of Aiden, I switched my attention to the other group members. I said, “Wow, I wasn’t expecting that.”

“I don’t know about you guys, but I don’t trust Aiden; you never know if he’s working for Morgan,” Nick said.

“Nick, I don’t think that he meant us any harm; his offer of assistance appeared to be made in good faith,” Ben says.

Lola gave Ben a nod and said, “I believe Ben is correct; I have a good feeling for him. Let’s not jump to conclusions.” I can’t help but think about Aiden as the gang calms down and unwind after their ordeal. I got a sense of recognition from him, and I couldn’t help but wonder if we would ever see him again.

“Is everything okay,” Maggie asked.

“Yeah, everything is good with us; please let us get cleaned up before you let Summer come to see us,” Ben said.

“Okay, she’s sleeping anyway.”

Everyone took their showers. Some even took the water hose to themselves, while Lola and I took our show in our private bathroom. By the time everyone was all cleaned up, Summer was awake. We were all in the living room by this time.

“Mama, Dada,” Summer called out as she entered the living room.

“Hey there, my baby girl, we are safe now.”

Maggie came out to see us. “Is she all taken care of?”

“Yes, we took her up to a cave in the mountain and sealed her in; we are all safe now. Oh, and I am now the owner of her throne; I am staying here in the mundane world because this is where my life is right now,” I say.

Maggie’s mouth dropped open in astonishment as she asked, “Wait, you did what? You escorted the queen of the Fae to a hidden cavern high in the mountains and imprisoned her there.”

“Yes, we did. It was the only way to protect ourselves and the rest of the world from her dictatorship, so we had no choice but to do it.”

"But that's completely insane!" There's no way you can lock up the queen or even a King like that; what about the repercussions?

I shrug, "After considering the possibilities, we concluded it was a good idea. More to the point, I am the legitimate heir to her throne, so it's not like we'll just let it sit empty."

Maggie shook her head, still trying to take everything in. "I find it hard to comprehend that you guys did this; if she finds a way to get out, she is going to be pissed and come after us again. What if someone finds out what you did?"

"No one will find out," Lola assured me with full conviction; we went to great lengths to conceal our track and ensure no proof was left behind. Even if somebody does finally figure out the truth, it won't make a difference in the end; we took the necessary precautions to safeguard not only ourselves but the people that we care about."

Maggie sighed, "Well, I guess that all that matters right now is ensuring everybody is safe."

"Exactly," Lola said, smiling. "And I'm sticking around in this boring world because this is where my life is. I have no use for the throne or the authority it bestows on its occupant. Just being able to go about my day with the people I care about."

"Can she come back?" Maggie asked.

"Unfortunately, there are ways that she can come back," I say.

About the Author

Born and raised in Port Jervis N.Y. and now living in Southern California.

This is my debut novel. I loved writing this book with all my heart.

Printed in the USA
CPSIA information can be obtained
at www.ICGtesting.com
LVHW041318110124
768681LV00029B/198

9 798869 029379